My Heart for Jill

The Mountain Mama Series

Blue Deco publishing
BlueDecoPublishing@gmail.com

My Heart For Jill
The Mountain Mama Series

Cover by Colleen Nye
Editing by Tate Publishing Enterprises
Formatting by Colleen Nye

Published by Blue Deco Publishing
PO BOX 1663 Royal Oak, MI 48068
BlueDecoPublishing@gmail.com

Copyright © 2016, 2018 Blue Deco Publishing & Marianne Waddill Wieland
Printed in the United States of America
Second Printing 2018

All rights reserved.

No part of this book may be reproduced or transmitted in any form or by any means, electronic or mechanical, including photocopying, recording or by any information storage and retrieval system, without written permission from the publisher.

The unauthorized reproduction or distribution of a copyrighted work is illegal. Criminal copyright infringement, including infringement without monetary gain, is investigated by the FBI and is punishable by fines and federal imprisonment.

This is a work of fiction. All characters and situations appearing in this work are fictitious. Any resemblance to real persons, living or dead, or personal situations is purely coincidental.

This book is dedicated to my mother, Lena Josephine Waddill and my grandmother, Annie K. Waddill. The character of Nana in this book is a combination of my mother and grandmother. Nana's character has the speech patterns and mannerisms of both and I grew up hearing these slang terms and accents.

My grandmother was a very big part of my childhood and she meant the world to me. Sadly, she passed away in 1977 at the age of ninety. At the time I wrote this book, my mother was ninety-five years old and we were still taking care of her as she had end stage Alzheimer's.

I am adding this dedication as the book is being reprinted by my new publisher and very sad to say, my mother passed away in January of 2017. Both would have loved this book and I just wanted to add this to give honor to them both.

One

"Where in tarnation is that man?!" Lorraine Dennison said as she paced faster and faster across the studio kitchen floor. The tap, tap, tapping of her mother's high heels was starting to wear on Jill's nerves. Her mother tended to be overly high strung when filming was due to begin of Jill's weekly show "Cooking Up a Storm."

Most of the family tended to be on the laid-back side, including Jill, but not Lorraine. Especially when everything was not going according to her lists and schedules. However, this was the first show of the second season and the guest chef had yet to appear.

Jill took a look around and everything was in place in her state of the art studio kitchen and ready for filming in her restaurant, "Mountain Mama's." Everything, that is, except Alphonse Laurant, this week's guest chef. Filming was set to begin in twenty minutes and Alphonse was to have arrived an hour ago.

"Mama, calm down" Jill said in her mild West Virginia accent. "We are West, by God, Virginians as Nana would say and everything will turn out fine. God always sees that things work out for the best according to *His* plans, not *ours*."

"I can't afford to calm down" said Lorraine. "When I spoke with Chef Laurant's agent on the phone, the agreement was that he would be here with plenty of time to be briefed on how the competition works. And, Jillian Marie Dennison, don't you dare preach to me. I get enough of that from my mother."

"Why did you hire him without a face to face meeting anyway? That is so unlike you" said Jill.

Lorraine stopped pacing and began to check her appearance in the closest mirror. She fussed a little with her perfectly coifed, bleached blonde hair and checked her teeth for lipstick smudges before she answered. "Well, I know that is out of character for me, but his reputation precedes him. He is the *best* French chef in New York City. Once he agreed, I set everything up with his agent. Besides, your father has met him and reckons he would make a great guest chef for the start of our new season."

Jill finished the final touches to her hair and makeup. "Mama, God never puts on us more than we can handle. He probably has a good reason for being this late. Maybe he wants to make some sort of grand entrance to show us all how important he is."

Jill's grandmother, Nana, came into the studio. "Land's sake, Lorraine. Quit a gettin' your too fancy britches all tied up in knots. He'll come in here a marchin' his high falutin' tukus in front of everbody just to show us hillbillies he's better'n we are. You mark my words." With that, Lena Josephine Marshall, or Nana, as the family called her, sauntered out of the room leaning on her cane.

"Hey y'all!" Jill's younger sister, Josie, came into the room leading a young girl by the arm. The girl couldn't be more than fifteen or sixteen by the look of her thought Jill. Her dark blond pony-tail sitting high on top of her head and stylish teenage clothing almost screamed she was from the city and, Jill would bet, not from a West Virginia city.

"Dad's running late so I'm going to start his four o'clock interview. This is Anika, by the way, and she is applying for that open position with the kitchen clean-up crew."

Josie saw her mother's annoyed look aimed in her direction and said, "I'm just going to chat a little until Dad gets here. You know, make her feel comfortable."

She looked at Anika. "Ain't that right honey? We'll be in the lounge if you need anything." Before she left the room, she said to her mother and sister. "By the way, Alphonse Laurant is drop dead gorgeous. Just wait until you see him." With that she left the studio dragging Anika behind her.

Jill didn't miss the wide-eyed stare on Anika's face as she left the room with Josie, but then, she was used to it from most customers who were not from around Beaumont, West Virginia, or not familiar with "Mountain Mama's restaurant. She took a last look in the mirror at herself and left the set to go say a quick prayer for a speedy entrance from 'Alphonse the Great.'

~

Nick Wallace was taking a leisurely stroll from Allen's Market where he had picked up a few things for his and his daughter's new home. Most of the food and non-food items were for her and his plan was to meet her at some restaurant called "Mountain Mama's" where she had a four o'clock interview for, he guessed, some sort of odd job. He was not convinced she had a good skill set to hold down a job unless the job in question was expensive clothing, chasing boys, or texting on the phone. Anyway, the place sounded like a dump to him but he was impressed that she had wanted to earn some money for herself. Up until now, she had shown no interest in moving to this place and had been punishing Nick for making her spend her last two years of high school in this 'po-dunk' town as she called it.

The last four years she had been living with his parents in the penthouse of the Grand Wallace New York, the hotel chain owned by his family. Since Nick was traveling most of the time scouting new locations for building and checking on the progress of new construction, he had seen no other choice but to leave his daughter in the hands of his parents, Margaret and Andrew Wallace. Of course, he knew Anika would be 'managed' mostly by a nanny and butler to make sure she had the necessities such as getting to school on time, had healthy meals, and did her homework. The less she was in his mother's company, the better.

Prior to four years ago, Anika had been raised by Nick's Aunt Bess in a small town about an hour from New York City. Aunt Bess had been a lifeline for Nick during most of the formative years of his youth and he had spent most of his life from the age of eight into his adulthood in her loving presence.

Aunt Bess was his mother's sister. She had lost her husband after only a few years of marriage and they were never blessed with children. Two people could not have been more different than his mother and his Aunt. Where his mother was arrogant, narcissistic, and intolerant of anyone whom she felt did not measure up to her standards, his Aunt Bess was a loving, hard- working, and nurturing Christian woman. His father was also very self-important and never had much to do with his children unless there was some benefit to the family business.

Aunt Bess had taken over the raising of Nick at her sister's request. His older brother had been sent away to boarding school in London and his younger sister and brother had been no trouble to the nanny. It was just Nick who posed a problem. He refused to stay in the background of his parent's lives and boarding school had been unsuccessful. Nick was gifted in playing the piano and his mother had asked her sister to raise Nick and try to facilitate this gift. Nick was not sure how his mother knew about his gift since she never bothered to come to a recital nor even listen to him play at home. And when she did happen to hear him practicing, it was to criticize. Most of her information about his wonderful talent was from his music teacher at school.

Aunt Bess was all too happy to do this and Nick was all too happy to go. It was there that Nick flourished on the piano and excelled at dance, a condition put forth by his aunt who had been a dance instructor throughout most of her life. However, unlike his parents who were always busy building their hotel empire and climbing the social ladder, Aunt Bess never let her dance classes over shadow Nick and his accomplishments.

Four years ago, Aunt Bess had stopped at a teller machine to withdraw some cash before going home. Anika had a field trip the following day and she wanted to make sure Anika had enough money for the gift shop. Aunt Bess was robbed at gun point by a drug crazed teenager who had no idea how to use a gun. He accidentally shot himself in the foot before accidentally shooting Aunt Bess in the abdomen. She died before the ambulance came. Not a day had passed that he didn't miss her and wish he could turn back time.

Aunt Bess had saved his daughter, as well, when Nick was sixteen and become involved with one of the girls in another dance class. This had ended in a pregnancy. The girl, Erica, a year older than Nick at the time, did not want the child. It was Aunt Bess that persuaded her to carry the child to term and also persuaded Nick's parents to pay Erica a substantial amount of money to do so, enough to finance the rest of Erica's dance training and any other training she might pursue. This, of course, caused an even bigger rift in the already strained relationship with his parents. He had never heard from Erica again, although, he had seen her name on Broadway a few times.

A car horn blared and Nick came back to the real world. He was across the street from a place that had "Mountain Mama's Restaurant and Studio" emblazoned across the home style entrance. It was a very large, two-story house-like structure made from rough-hewn wood, logs and decorative stones with a smaller wing, less impressive, to the right. There was a stone path to the front door with perfectly landscaped flowers, bushes and grasses. There was, also, a large deck with rocking chairs and benches placed in groups for, he supposed, the overflow of customers. The place was impressive, so okay, it was not a dump.

Nick decided to wait inside with his bag of groceries and hope his presence did not embarrass his daughter. It had begun to do so ever since she had been living with his parents.

He entered the front door and noticed some benches to his right. He sat down with his grocery bag and began to check his cell phone for messages or texts. Anika had said she would let him know when she was finished.

"There you are!"

He saw a short, big haired, blonde woman rushing toward him. He looked over his shoulder in case he was not the intended target.

"Get off your duff and quickly follow me. We're on the air in six minutes!" She started walking away then noticed his grocery bag. "I hope you haven't been looking through that bag. It's against the rules, you know."

She grabbed his arm and started pulling him off the bench.

"*I have been crazy with worry*! Do you know how frantic everyone has been waiting for you?!" She was moving at a slow jog and waving her arms around as she continued to reprimand him, so the *crazy part*, he could believe.

Nick kept up with her the best he could and tried to speak.

"Miss, I think you've got..."

Jill saw them coming and thought drop dead gorgeous was an understatement. She yelled loud enough for him to hear.

"Get over here *NOW* so I can brief you."

Nick tried again. "Now wait a minute..."

The short blond woman all but pushed him behind what appeared to be a kitchen setting surrounded by cameramen and other equipment and crew. Someone put a white apron on him from behind and a chef's hat on his head. His grocery bag was set to his left side.

Some older lady with a tight, gray perm and leaning on a cane came to stand in front of him. She lowered her glasses to look up at him.

"Well if it isn't Mr. Fancy Pants. What in the Sam Hill made you think you could trot yerself in here this late? Famous French Chef or not... I declare..." and just like that, she wandered off.

Nick looked to his right and his mouth dropped open. He could not have gotten words out if he tried. He supposed this woman must be Mountain Mama. She was taller than average, maybe 5'9" or so with big bones or muscles, he couldn't tell. She was wearing what looked like a tablecloth with arms, the red and white checkered kind. White? He couldn't tell that either since it looked fifty years old and was in need of a good washing. For that matter, the whole woman was in need of a good washing. Her grayish brown hair was sticking out like her head had been tazed and she was missing two or three teeth in the front.

What on Earth had he wandered, or been pushed, into he thought. Maybe even said out loud. Who could tell with all the noise and activity going on around him.

The short blonde lady appeared on his other side giving some kind of instructions.

"Now it goes like this...Jill, sorry, Mountain Mama, will introduce you and when the clock starts you will have one minute to make a game plan and forty-five minutes to cook a supper with all the ingredients in your grocery bag that has been provided by our crew. Your agent informed me that you understood the rules and were prepared for the battle."

With that, she moved to the other side of the kitchen area.

Someone else appeared from behind and patted his face down with powder. *He was going on television. Live. It dawned on him all of a sudden! This was a cooking show and they were expecting some French Chef to compete with this... this... hillbilly nightmare! He had to get out of there! He had to get out of there quick before... too late!*

The cameraman was counting down and country music started playing. The old lady to his right started doing a sort of hillbilly hip hop dance. She put on a wide toothless smile and started loudly talking to the camera.

"Welcome to 'Cooking Up a Storm' with me, Mountain Mama!"

Nick heard loud shouting and clapping, but due to the bright lights and activity had not noticed a small studio audience. Mountain Mama continued.

"What a treat we have for y'all today! We're startin' our second season with guest chef Alfonse Laurant from Marcel's in New York City!"

He heard louder shouts and clapping. Then he heard a funny buzzing in his ears. *No! No! No! This cannot be happening!*

Of all the chefs in the world, not Alfonse Laurant! Marcel's was the signature restaurant in the Grand Wallace New York. All he could think of was *"kill me now!"*

Two

Jill continued her dance and looked to Alphonse who appeared about ready to faint. *Strange.* She had heard of his reputation for being the best of the best in French cuisine but also his love for the camera. Oh, and his foul temper. *Drop dead gorgeous* didn't even begin to describe this man. He was tall, at least six-foot four inches, with broad shoulders and a trim waist. At least what she could see. His hair was dark brown, short, with that 'messy-look' that was so popular these days and took a lot of work to achieve. His eyes were dark blue and it wouldn't take much for her to get lost in them. Okay, that was corny!

Hmm… he looks familiar. She thought for a minute. He looks a lot like that actor that plays the medical officer in those space frontier movies that she was such a fan of. The newer movies, of course. She had to give herself a mental shake. She had to get back into character and quick. The cameras were rolling.

"It's so good to have y'all here, Alphonse, to start the new season off with a darn tootin' good French supper!" She continued. "So ye think ye can beat ol' Mountain Mama with all that fancy French food in yer grocery bag, do ye?"

French and supper? *Was it legal to use both words in the same sentence* thought Nick? Mountain Mama was looking at him. He was starting to sweat. Big time. He realized she was expecting him to say or do something, but with the buzzing in his ears and all the bright lights, he was having a hard time just understanding her 'mountain lingo'. And her voice was like fingernails on a chalkboard.

"How 'bout it Alphonse? Er'e ye ready to beat the britches off this ol' lady?" Jill noticed he was white as a sheet and holding himself up against the kitchen counter. *Something was terribly wrong.* Maybe he was sick. She moved over close to him pretending to adjust his chef's hat and said so only he could hear.

"Dude, say something. We've got to get this show going."

"What?" He whispered back to her while wiping sweat from his forehead.

"Anything. The sooner we get this started, the sooner we'll finish," said Jill.

Funny, thought Nick. The old lady had a whole different voice tone speaking personally to him.

Jill looked him square in the eyes, but noticed how far she had to look up. "Dude, just flow with it. I'll lead, you follow, okay?"

Nick gave a slight nod and swallowed hard to beat down the sudden nausea. In for a penny, in for a pound, as his Aunt Bess would say. So he did the only thing he could do in this situation. He swallowed again and jumped in with both feet.

In what he hoped was a French accent, he said "Eet ees my pleasure to 'elp with your heelbeely ruse."

Jill whipped her head towards him and narrowed her eyes. That was the fakest French accent she had ever heard. Actually, it sounded more like a combination of French and....what? Turkish? And maybe a little bit of New York?

"Well, well, well." Jill drew out each 'well'. "I believe we got us a good 'un today folks! I think Alphonse must be from the 'Bronx' of France."

The audience started laughing and clapping.

"At least I am not from ze Dog Patch or punkin' patch or some kind of patch to be zure," Nick countered.

Jill's only response, barely noticeable, was a short intake of breath. *Here we go,* she thought, *another stuck up man who thought all West Virginians were 'hillbillies'.* But to be fair, her costume as Mountain Mama didn't help. Her character was not to portray West Virginians in a hillbilly way, but it was a character created by her Nana when the restaurant first opened five years ago. Nana had acted as hostess. Health issues had forced her to step down. When she did, Jill took the character into the kitchen, where she was chef, to continue to honor the original Mountain Mama, her Nana, for whom the restaurant was named.

Lorraine appeared on camera and took control.

"Mountain Mama and Alphonse will now unpack their grocery bags and will have one minute to make a game plan. They may also use any of the ingredients provided in our studio pantry and fridge behind them. You may start unpacking...NOW." With that, Lorraine stepped out of camera range.

Jill began to unpack her bag. Her little brother, Matt, usually stocked the grocery bags and always tried to stump her with unusual ingredients. Today she unpacked mangoes, eggplant, pork loin, red cabbage, potato sticks, raisins, rhubarb, cottage cheese and creamed corn. Okay, she could work with that and she began to organize and add to her grocery bag, ingredients from the pantry.

Nick, on the other hand, knew what was in his bag since he had just picked the items up earlier, most of them being for his daughter. He was very reluctant to unpack it. Either way, he would be jeopardizing this show more than he had already if he did not do something to move forward. So reluctantly, he unpacked boxed macaroni and cheese, peanut butter, strawberry jelly, peach flavored Greek yogurt, Oreo's, frozen pizza rolls, pretzels, a hammer, shampoo, panty hose, and bird seed.

Jill was speechless, but only for about five seconds. "Well, that there is *some kind'a* foreign French food folks. You seen it here first! Just think, you lucky judges will get to sample this fine French dee-light!"

Boy, just wait until she found Matt. He had gone too far this time. She heard someone from the sidelines stand up and yell.

"I think ye might be a wantin' to jerk a knot in somebody's rump for what's in yer bag there, Alphonse, you good lookin' piece of French finery!"

Of course, that came from Nana and was loud enough for the audience to hear.

Nick felt the red creeping up his face and had no idea what to try to cook with the items he had to work with.

Aunt Bess would say, *your best defense is to go on the offense if you are backed into a corner.*

"Zo, vhat are *you* making? Stuffed Possum Zupreem? Vait!" He looked around wildly. "I don't zee ze possum! 'ere you go. You can use ze hammer to catch zat one I zaw out on ze back porch."

He picked up the hammer just in case she took him up on the offer. For all he knew, it wouldn't surprise him if there was a possum on the back porch.

Lorraine was fanning herself from a chair and Nana called out, standing once again.

"Now I'd like to see that!" The audience was laughing.

"What are *you* a plannin' to cook with yer bird seed and panty hose...suet?" Jill had both hands on her hips.

Both were staring at each other when Jill's father, Jim Dennison, a totally white-haired man, even though he was only in his fifties, walked up with Josie and a young girl.

"What did I miss? It's awful loud out here." He looked up at Nick. "Who's that?"

Just then Anika stepped forward. "Dad?"

Three

What had he told himself earlier? Oh yeah, he wanted to keep from embarrassing his daughter. Well, that ship had sailed.

Mountain Mama spoke loudly. "Times a wastin'." She looked at Nick. "Let's start cookin' up a storm!"

The music started back up and Mountain Mama started that hillbilly tap dance thing again, but he noticed she was writing something on a piece of paper. She passed it to him and he read "Live show. Can't break. Cook something. NOW!"

He looked out at his daughter who was sitting at a table with her head down on her crossed arms. The old lady was seated next to her patting her on the back. He looked over at Mountain Mama and started bobbing his head up and down like he was trying to dance with her.

"I'm not Alphonse," he whispered.

Jill stopped dancing and shouted with her hands in the air.

"Shocker!"

She realized a second too late that everyone else had heard her obnoxious statement as well. She did the only thing she could think of to fix it.

"Look at you, you good lookin' French son of a gun over here a tryin' to flirt with me!"

Nick's eyes nearly popped out of their sockets and he backed away from her quickly, knocking half of his supplies to the floor.

Jill continued at his expense.

"Wouldn't be the first time I've had to fend off the fellers after this purty face!" She gave him a big wink and started hamming it up for the camera.

Nick could feel his face on fire as he began to pick up his groceries. He braved another look at his daughter and saw that she was starting to laugh along with the rest of the audience. She seemed to be enjoying his mortification. No surprise there.

Lorraine had rallied and was approaching them at their kitchen stations. Nick figured he could not possibly have looked any more ridiculous than he did at that moment, so he made the decision to join in with the hilarity and spirit of the show. After all, what did he have to lose? Well, for one, his dignity. Oh, and a possible law suit from Alphonse Laurant.

He could cook macaroni and cheese and make pizza rolls so he started a pot to boil the water and turned on the oven. He saw Lorraine stop at Mountain Mama's station.

"What will you be cooking up for us today Mountain Mama?" asked Lorraine.

"Well, Lo-raine, thank ye fer askin'" Mountain Mama emphasized each syllable. "I'm a gonna cook up some pork chops with a rhubarb sauce, some fancy slaw, and a side dish of eggplant and taters using the tater sticks. I'm, also, a gonna bake up some of my special corn bread with the creamed corn. It's a gonna be a dandy!"

Lorraine made a point of looking at each thing Mountain Mama pointed out. "That sounds so yummy Mountain Mama! I'm sure our judge's mouths are just watering waiting for a taste."

"Now I'm a startin' by takin' my fancy kitchen hatchet." She waved it in the air. "And a choppin' up this hunk," she looked straight at Nick and landed a loud chop through the pork loin, "of meat."

"I see," said Lorraine looking from Jill to Nick. "That's going to be a real Mountain Mama treat for our judges."

Lorraine moved hesitantly over to Nick's area as he was adding the macaroni to the boiling water and putting the pizza rolls in the oven. "Now, Alphonse, what kind of tasty French treats will you be presenting to our judges today? And remember you have to use everything in your grocery bag."

Nick's eyes began to shift back and forth over his items. He opened his mouth to speak but for the life of him, nothing would come out. He glanced, again, out at his daughter and saw her eyes were narrowed and she had a nasty smirk on her face. She, too, knew most of what was in the bag since she had put the items on his grocery list. She was loving his misery. *Well, two could play this game.*

"Lorraine, my turtle dove, I am making ze pasta zuprise of my country zo loved by ze children all over ze France." He muttered under his breath. "It'll be a surprise if it's edible. I vill, then, make a dipping sauce from ze jelly and some cayenne pepper to give it ze kick. I vill, also, be making ze dessert zat ees, how you say, to die for!"

"Okay then, how interesting that sounds." Lorraine drew out the words looking over his items with an obvious question on her face. "Alphonse, what will you be doing with the non-edible items from your grocery bag?"

"Lorraine, I am glad you asked zat question." Nick grabbed her hand, made a low bow and kissed it with a loud smack. "Gracias for asking!" The audience howled with laughter. "Vat did I zay?!"

Nick looked at Lorraine who was looking shocked and in need of a chair. She looked over at Mountain Mama hoping for some words of wisdom. All Nick and Lorraine heard was Mountain Mama call him a 'knucklehead.' The audience howled louder.

Nick continued, "As I vas saying before, I vill vash my hands now vith zees zhampoo."

"But Alphonse," Lorraine interrupted. "You have already started to work with the food. Shouldn't you wash your hands before you start?"

"Oui, oui, oui," stated Nick, "but in my country, ve start ze cooking process and zen ve vash vith zees shampoo." He looked at the name on the bottle, "Zhampoo du Zuave. Vee find eet zaves time zat vay."

Lorraine looked at the camera speechless.

Nick continued, "vith ze hammer I vill crush ze cookies and ze pretzels for ze dessert." He began to pound with the hammer making a huge mess all over the counter.

Mountain Mama came back with "Will ye be a addin' in the birdseed too?"

"Nein, Nein, Nein!" Nick gestured wildly with his arms scattering cookies, pretzels, and seed all over the sink and floor. He noticed the audience was doubling over with laughter and his daughter was almost rolling in the aisle she was laughing so hard. He couldn't help but think what the real Alphonse would do if he ever got wind of this fiasco. Thankfully, it was aired only locally. He hoped.

"Ze bird seed I will put een ze panty hose like zis." He poured the bird seed down one leg of the panty hose and cut the leg off with the kitchen shears. He tied the hose in a knot to form a medium sized ball of seed.

"Zis vill make clean up zo easy you vill vant to use all zee time!" He demonstrated by squirting some shampoo on the counter, soaking the bird seed and panty hose combination. He began to wipe down the counter making a slimy, soapy mess.

"Zee, eet ees magnifico!" Nick took a dramatic bow and waved to the audience. He got thunderous applause and a standing ovation for his effort. He looked at Mountain Mama who was shaking her head at him but he thought he saw her trying hard not to laugh. He also heard her whisper.

"Dude, get your plates together. Quick!" And then he possibly heard her say 'moron'.

As Nick began to get his plates together, he noticed the white-haired man reading a letter off to the side. He showed it to Lorraine who began to shake it in the old lady's face. The old lady just shrugged her shoulders and went back to her seat. Lorraine visibly wilted, but her look towards him was one of utter shock.

"Snap out of it." Nick heard the white-haired man say in an angry voice to Lorraine. "This show still has to go on and I have to make a phone call. Quick!"

Lorraine rallied again and called the three audience judges to the front. Nick saw a table set with silverware and water glasses for three people. If he was a praying man...no, he was never going down that road again. No one was listening anyway, at least, not to him.

Nick hurriedly slopped some way too chewy macaroni and cheese on three plates making a hole in the middle. He filled the hole with a big glob of peanut butter. His pizza rolls were burned but, he thought, still edible. He watered down the strawberry jelly with pancake syrup and added the cayenne pepper for the dipping sauce. He scraped the hammered cookies and pretzels in the peach yogurt and added some of each to all three plates.

Lorraine gave a one minute warning and Nick looked over at Mountain Mama to see her plates were done. She had her hands on her ample looking hips and was looking at him with a look that could only be described as...well, there were no words to describe how she was looking at him.

At the last minute, he decided to put a few drops of jelly around his macaroni wreath and finished just as Lorraine called the end of the competition.

"Time! Step away from your plates!"

Nick stepped back from the food, but as he did, he grabbed a handful of the bird seed, throwing it over his shoulder. "For good luck!"

Jill was happy with her food presentation and didn't know whether to laugh or cry at what 'Alphonse' had put together. *Lord,* she prayed silently, *if this is the end of my show, please grant me the strength to see it through. Oh, and if you could, the grace to deal with this imposter.*

Jill put on her Mountain Mama toothless smile and grabbed a handful of bird seed as well. She hammed it up for the audience throwing it over her shoulder as Nick had done.

"Fer good luck." She looked over at Nick and said quietly so only he could hear. "You're going to need it!"

Four

An hour and a half later Nick was sitting at a table running his fingers through his hair and rubbing his exhausted eyes. He could see Mountain Mama standing in a group with Lorraine, the white haired man, Josie and the old lady. The man seemed particularly upset with the old lady. He kept shaking a piece of paper at her but she kept a blank expression. Lorraine was trying to calm the man down without much success. Mountain Mama was alternately trying to calm the man as well as Lorraine and at the same time trying to shelter the old lady from the attack. Mountain Mama seemed to give up and put both arms around the old lady. The old lady's face transformed from blank, then began to shed a few tears. He could hear Mountain Mama talking softly.

"It's okay Nana, it's okay. We all know you didn't mean to cause a problem. You just forgot the letter was in your purse. It'll all be okay. You'll see. The Lord will work it all out". She continued to pat the old woman on the back.

Nick had survived the judging of his and Mountain Mama's meals for thirty more minutes after the 'good luck' birdseed toss. He had thought the show would never end once the judges started with their comments.

Of course, Mountain Mama won. The two female judges who looked to be in their forties with big hair and too many teeth gave him praise for his dessert. Since Mountain Mama had not prepared a dessert, they had no comparison. Mostly, they just batted their eyelashes and one even winked at him.

The little old man who was the third judge, spat Nick's food on the floor and declared it a disaster. He loudly proclaimed that Marcel's, in New York City, would not be a place in which he would ever eat. Not as long as Alphonse Laurant was chef.

The two ladies said they were looking forward to a trip to New York City to eat at Marcel's and see what else Alphonse had they could sample. They had worked hard to try to make their intentions clear as to what they were really interested in and it clearly was not the food. It briefly flitted through his mind how many, if any, of the people from this small West Virginia town had or would ever travel to New York City. However, the way the two ladies kept looking him up and down, he would not be surprised if they did, indeed, show up at his door one day.

Nick saw Anika coming his way and braced himself for another attack.

"Dad," she said. "You were awesome! At first I was so embarrassed that you would try to humiliate me in this way, but I think you did more damage to yourself!"

"I was not trying to embarrass you, myself, or anyone". Nick stood up, hands on the edge of the table.

"I simply came here to pick you up after your interview when…" She interrupted and grabbed his arm.

"Guess what? They want to hire me! Can you believe it?"

No. He could not.

"They might even let me play my violin."

Here? In this rustic place? The violin?

Anika continued. "They have live entertainment on the weekends and some week nights. They even have their own family band! The whole family plays and everything!"

Nick sat back down. Anika started to whine and beg. "Please, please, please! Say it's okay!" She folded her hands in a prayer fashion and continued.

"I promise it won't interfere with my school work."

Nick wasn't sure how to respond. He scratched his head with both hands in an irritated manner before he answered.

"Anika, let me ask you a question. Why, all of a sudden, do you want a job? You have never expressed any interest in a job before now. You won't even wash a dish or clean your room without the threat of being grounded. What gives?"

"Well dad," Anika began as she sat opposite Nick. "Maybe this will teach me some responsibility. Maybe I'm growing up more than you realize. Maybe it'll show you I can handle my own car. Maybe..."

She was getting more and more animated as Nick cut her off. "Is having your own car what this is all about? I can take you to and from school and if you do start working here, you can walk."

"You don't get it, do you dad? I am *almost seventeen* now. Having my own car would help me be able to come and go when I want. Without having to depend on you.

Are you really going to leave the job site twice a day to take me and pick me up from school? The job site is twelve miles away. Or I could use your Jag."

When he didn't respond she went on. "You took me away from my home, my friends, *my school* to a place in the middle of nowhere to spend the next two years of my life. I have nothing and I have no one!"

"Excuse me, Miss Thing." Nick was starting to get really angry. "No one? What am I?" He continued, louder than he should. "What happened to the little girl that used to love the simple life when she lived with Aunt Bess? Has the last four years living with your grandmother corrupted your thinking that much that you have forgotten the values on which you were raised?!"

Some of the fight seemed to leave Nick. "I knew it was a bad idea to move you in with my parents after Aunt Bess died. I felt it in my gut."

Anika crossed her arms and sat back, changing her tactics. "Why *did* you leave me there dad? Why *didn't* you just take me with you?"

He couldn't believe she was going down that road again. Piling on the guilt. *How many more times would he have to explain this to her?*

"Because I was basically doing three jobs at the same time. My parents had been putting the pressure on me to take on more work for the family business scouting for new hotel sites and over-seeing the construction. They felt my concert tours were a frivolous waste of time, but I had contracts that couldn't be broken. The tour would last another six months which would require travel all over the United States and Europe. I was not going to drag a twelve year old girl through that. You had been through enough losing Aunt Bess."

"So instead, I lost my father. I really needed you, dad, and you let me down." Anika's eyes were filled with tears that he knew she would not let fall.

"I was there as often as possible. I was also taking care of Aunt Bess's estate. I had hoped my mother would help, but I guess we were lucky she even came to the funeral."

For Nick, that had been the worst year of his life. The fear of leaving his precious daughter with grandparents that had not even wanted to see her when she was growing up. His sister, Gwen, had been nearby and had helped in the early days following the funeral. She was the manager of the Grand Wallace New York so she could be counted on to help Anika through her early teenage 'girl problems'.

Aunt Bess had left everything to Nick and Anika. That, along with his earnings from the concert tours alone, would leave them set for life.

After that time, he had thrown himself into his work and Anika had done the same. She excelled at everything she did but was particularly gifted on the violin. Aunt Bess had started her with lessons at the age of five. The same age he had started playing the piano. He had graduated from Julliard and he guessed Anika would do the same.

After that concert tour ended, he had gone into more work for the family and less on tour. He still played several times per year, but he found he enjoyed project management as well.

"As I said, that was no life for a child, and I stand by my decision." Nick was not as sure of that decision as he was letting on to his daughter. He did not know if her attitude was from being with his parents the last four years or normal teenage drama. He did, however, know his mother's influence had not been good.

"Well, I am not a child now, dad, and I have become used to a certain way of life. We are rich, but are living in the sticks. No bright lights. No theaters or museums. No designer clothing stores. How can I live like that? If I want any half way decent clothing, I was told I would have to go into Beckley and that is twenty miles from here!" She stood up. "Why can't you understand my side of anything?!"

He stood when he noticed Josie heading their way. "We are going to have to table this discussion for another time. I think someone else wants to talk to us."

Josie stopped and said something to Mountain Mama then came over to their table. She looked at Anika. "So, what's the verdict sweetheart? Will you be able to take the job?"

Nick looked at them both. What a contrast they were. Josie with her soft blonde curls, big brown eyes, and genuine smile and Anika with her overly made up face, designer clothes, and a smile as phony as Nick's French accent. Something was not right here. He was sure there was some ulterior motive in Anika's insistence in working here. Sooner or later he would find out what it was.

"Okay," said Nick. "Okay. But if your grades suffer, then you will have to quit. Is that clear Anika?"

"Crystal clear, dad. My grades will remain outstanding as always. I promise. And I will keep up with my violin practice as well." She smiled sweetly at Josie.

"Okay then," said Josie. "Let's go fill out some paperwork. I'll go ahead and handle it. I think my dad and sister want to talk to you about the show, so don't leave yet." She stopped and turned back to Nick. "Oh, and you were so great, I think you should do another show!" And with that, she flounced away with Anika.

Nick began to rub his temples again. He had a dull throbbing starting up behind his eyes. He looked up to see Mountain Mama, the white haired man, Lorraine and the old lady heading towards him. The man and Mountain Mama looked angry at Lorraine and the old lady. Lorraine looked like she wanted to run and the old lady had another blank look on her face. He was the one that should be angry and he certainly was! They had better not try to pin this on him. He had been an innocent bystander.

He saw them all stop before they got to his table and start arguing again, but this time their anger seemed more towards Lorraine rather than the old lady. He hoped he could hold it together and not cause any further humiliation to himself so he and his daughter could get out of here. He needed an end to this disaster of a day.

Mountain Mama started heading his way again but the rest of the group sat down at a table near the kitchen but still within hearing distance.

Then he saw it! Anika's ulterior motive! Nick had had enough! Just as Mountain Mama reached him, Nick jumped up and all but screamed at her

"Who is that?!" He pointed at a young man walking towards the seated group at the other table.

Jill had expected confrontation but *what was this?* "*That* is my little brother, Matt. He works in the kitchen too. As a matter of fact, my whole family works here. Why? What's the problem?" She was leaning towards Nick with her hands on her hips.

Nick felt himself losing control. He had known that Anika had an agenda for wanting to work here. He should have known a boy would be involved.

"Your brother?" He yelled. "He looks more like your grandson! He can't possibly be your brother! Who was your father... Noah?"

Nick looked like he might explode. "No, I don't buy that at all!" Nick could feel his blood pressure rising.

What is this man's problem, thought Jill. "Okay," she said. "Time out dude." He looked like steam would start rolling out of his ears at any minute.

Jill continued. "Don't you yell at me and don't bring my brother into this." She could feel her family's eyes on them with Lorraine looking particularly uncomfortable and fidgety.

"*You* get on *my* TV show pretending to be someone you're not, make a royal mess of my kitchen, and clown around like an idiot on a *live* show! We can't edit it or cut it out! Do you have any understanding of what you have done?"

"What I've done? Do you have any idea of what you've done?" Nick was not yelling but somehow the words had more bite to them than if he had been.

"I came in here earlier to meet my daughter." He saw Mountain Mama looked startled and saw her eyes widen. "Yes, my daughter, after she had a four o'clock interview for a job. I was grabbed by that short female dynamo over there." He pointed at Lorraine.

"No one bothered to ask my name and I couldn't get a word in before I was pushed in front of a camera and announced I was Alphonse Laurant. It is painfully obvious that you don't know him!" Nick was pounding his fist on the table but couldn't stop himself. He was on a roll. "Alphonse Laurant, of all people on the planet, Alphonse Laurant!"

"Maybe you should just calm down." Jill saw her mother get up and try to leave the room but her father made her sit back down. Nick's face was red and she was afraid he was going to have a stroke or something.

Nick started up again. "I can't even believe someone like Alphonse Laurant would agree to come to a place like this!" He waved his arms around encompassing most of the surrounding area.

Jill was starting to get a good picture of this guy. She narrowed her eyes at Nick.

"And what, pray tell, is wrong with my restaurant. Is Alphonse too good for us West Virginia hillbillies?"

"Alphonse Laurant is the most conceited, arrogant jerk on the face of the Earth! I contend he would not come all the way from New York City to Beaumont, West Virginia to compete in a cooking competition with a toothless old bat! I don't think you could pay him enough!"

Nick started waving his arms around. "This place reeks of hillbilly to the max! I feel like I need to whip out a banjo and start a hootenanny just to be in the building!"

"That could be arranged," said Jill through clenched teeth.

Nick wasn't finished. He knew he had gone too far but he couldn't seem to stop himself.

"Then the show started and I was forced, *forced I say*, to go along with it!"

"Then you!" He pointed at Jill's nose. "You started that hillbilly hip hop." Nick demonstrated by doing a tap dance shuffle, waving his arms all around. He began imitating Jill.

"Hi y'all! I'm Mountain flippin' Mammy!"

By this time the rest of the family had joined Jill and were all just staring at Nick. Jill could see him visibly deflate right in front of them.

Nick realized he had done it now. Mountain Mama was going to let him have it. He could see it in her eyes.

Jill wasn't sure if she wanted to punch him or imitate him in return. *Toothless old bat did he say?* Jill let out a belly laugh that startled them all. Once she started laughing, she couldn't stop. She saw Nick wilt into his seat and she tried to get the laughter under control, she really did. She sat down across from him but every time she tried to speak she started laughing all over again.

Nick had gone a little pale. Nana jumped in.

"'Ere ye sick young'un? Ye know, we can get ye Jill's banjo if ye really want to play it fer us."

Lorraine took her mother by the arm and said, "I don't think he feels well. Let's just let him be for now."

"Ye know what's wrong don't ye? I knowed what's wrong right off, I did." Nana poked at Nick's chest. "Ye've got the botts."

Nick sat up again. "The whats?"

"The botts," Jill said. "That's West Virginia for 'you're sick and don't know what's wrong'. "At least that's what we all think it means. It's Nana's word for what ails you".

Lorraine led her mother away.

Nick said, "I've had more than I can take for one day and now that old biddy tells me I've got 'the botts'. That is rich!"

Jill was starting to get very irritated at Nick again. "I realize now that we have put you in a very awkward situation. We will totally accept the blame, but that is no reason for you to take it out on Nana. She may be indirectly to blame for why this happened but she has a medical condition that causes problems that we sometimes cannot control." Jill continued. "I apologize for all of this and I think we need to sit down and discuss it when we have all had some rest."

Nick could not seem to formulate a response at that point. The white-haired man stepped forward.

"I'm Jim Dennison, Jill's father."

Who was this 'Jill' they kept mentioning? He stood and weakly shook Jim's hand.

Jim continued. "How about you and your daughter come by the restaurant tomorrow around six in the evening. We'll all have some supper and sort out this whole unfortunate incident. Jill and I will be able to figure out what needs to be done. I still don't really understand how this happened. It would be nice for me to go through it again from your point of view if you would be willing to help me with that."

Jim had walked him a few paces towards the door where Anika was waiting. Jim was earnestly waiting for his reply.

"Will that old bat be joining us?" Nick pointed to Mountain Mama and knew he should feel some shame in his comment. She probably couldn't help the missing teeth. Maybe they had no dental plan at this place. But surely she could get to a bar of soap and some water!

"No. Not exactly," said Jim. "But Jill *is* the owner and chef. She will work this out with you. So, will you come?"

"Sure. Sure." Nick spoke weakly and with that, he walked out the door hoping Anika was following.

Five

"I've never seen someone cut such a shine!" Jill absently scratched her forehead where her wig was tickling her.

The group made their way back to the kitchen area. Jill thought she had seen it all but Nick put on quite a show. And imitating her! He looked like he was doing a real tap dance there for a minute.

"You know," she said. "With some work, I think I could have him doing some clogging."

"That was quite the dance he did," said Jim. "I still can't believe he called you a toothless old bat."

"He sure took a dislike to me," said Jill.

She removed her wig and put her feet up on a chair. Then she took a napkin and started removing the black makeup she had put on her teeth.

Josie patted her hand. "I can't believe that. Everyone loves you, sis. He hasn't been here long, only two weeks. Anika said he hand-picked this area because of the people and slower way of life. I think he just hasn't been here long enough to shake off all that city glitter of his. It'll happen, you just mark my words."

Jim had been staring at Jill and got a sudden look of realization on his face.

"I know what happened," he said to Jill. "That man didn't realize you were playing a part. He thinks you really are an old lady. You are believable as one but that is just bad manners to call someone you don't even know such unkind names. I think he'll see things differently once he's had some rest and time to think this over."

"His daughter was really sweet," said Josie.

"Must take after her mother," said Jill sarcastically.

"Well, I don't care," said Josie. "Anika is a doll and she really wants to work here. You know, she's been playing the fiddle for years and I was thinking she could sit in with us sometime on one of our family practices. We're gonna need another fiddle player when Matt goes to college next year. She said she'd be glad to stop by here after school and practice some with Matt."

"Did I hear someone say my name?" Matt crossed the room carrying a plate of fried chicken and cornbread.

"I was just telling Mom and dad about Anika offering to come by and practice the fiddle with you," said Josie.

"She just joined the orchestra at school and she is *really* good. But I don't think she has played any of our music before. No country. No gospel. All she has to do though is hear something one time or read through the music and she's got it down pat."

Matt started to eat the chicken then paused. "I think she could teach me a thing or two. I need to be working more on her kind of classical music. Not that I can't play it already, but I wouldn't mind a few tips from her. Just think, dad, this time next year I'll be in New York at Julliard!" He continued to eat his chicken without waiting for a response.

Jim addressed them all. "We should probably eat too. I'll go and make sure Nana is okay." He stood up and then paused. "I still can't believe how this whole thing happened. Lorraine just gets too wound up when any little thing goes wrong with her plans."

"I know dad," said Jill. "But I should have stepped in myself and at least verified his name. It's just that..."

She paused the rushed ahead. "Josie said he was gorgeous and when mom dragged him in, well, let's just say, I thought it was Alphonse as well." She grabbed a piece of Matt's chicken but didn't start to eat it. "Poor Nana," she continued. "She's getting worse dad. We've got to keep her away from the mail. None of this would have happened if we had seen that letter when it came two weeks ago."

"I called Mr. Laurant's agent and he thinks it would be best if we keep all this from Alphonse. Since the show is only aired locally, I think we will be fine" said Jim. "We can sort it out tomorrow when Mr. Wallace and his daughter join us for supper. I'll see you all later. I have to get your mom and Nana home."

He kissed each of his daughter's cheeks and ruffled Matt's hair. He proceeded to the rear of the building and mounted the stairs leading to the second floor.

Josie took a piece of Matt's cornbread and stood up.

"Quit eating my food!" said Matt. "I'm on duty in half an hour and I need sustenance. I'm still a growing boy!"

He grabbed the chicken from Jill just as she was taking a bite and made a grab for the cornbread but Josie took off at a jog towards the restaurant area.

"Hey! I was going to eat that!" griped Jill.

"Yeah, but do you really need it?" He playfully punched her on the shoulder and took off after Josie leaving Jill at the table alone.

Matt is right, she thought. Even though she knew her family meant no harm, she was still sensitive about her weight. By the media's standards she was probably considered 'plus size'. But she was comfortable with her looks and was not about to starve herself to be 'model thin' just to be accepted by the opposite sex. Or accepted by anyone. She had taken some hard knocks to get to where she was today. She felt good about herself. At five foot, nine inches and a solid size thirteen, she did the best she could with what she had to work with. She was confident in how she dressed, how she ran her restaurant, her cooking, and even as Mountain Mama.

So, how come she had been so unsuccessful in relationships with the male gender? When she thought about it, she really hadn't put that much effort into it. She had focused mainly on her career. She'd had a few boyfriends when she was younger but she'd had only one serious relationship in her thirty-one years and that was a disaster. No, she wasn't going to think about that this late in the day. Today was enough of a disaster by itself.

She started slowly walking up to her suite of rooms on the second floor. When she felt down, which was rare, she tried to focus on her accomplishments instead of any failures. She had graduated from high school with honors and had been accepted into a renowned culinary school where she spent the next few years working and studying in other countries. A year in Italy, a year in France and even a year in Japan. She had learned a lot, but she had missed her family terribly and missed the simple life offered by her small West Virginia home town. So, she had returned home a confident, financially successful but lonely, young woman.

Her plans all along were to open her own restaurant. She had been lucky to have found a huge old barn in her home town that was due to be demolished. She had bought it for a pittance and with the help of her family, and the remodeling company she had hired out of Beckley, she had turned it into a large restaurant. With two floors, this offered her enough space for her living quarters, two large meeting rooms and two smaller ones. She booked the rooms out for weddings, reunions, business meetings or for any group that wanted the special attention she and her family were known to give. They even offered theme dinners.

All in all, she was very happy with her life. It was too bad some people couldn't separate her as a person with the place she called home.

She reached her area of the second floor. There she showered and changed into soft orange Capri pants and a white tank top. She combed out her dark auburn hair that came just below her ears and put in her amber colored contacts. There was still time for a walk in the park.

West Virginia in September was still very warm but the temperature could drop quite a bit when the sun dipped behind the mountains. She grabbed an old hoodie and was headed out the door when Josie stopped her.

"I figured you would head to the park after this day just to unwind a little. I don't think you got to eat either, so I fixed you a sandwich and some tea to take with you." She handed Jill the basket. "Try to enjoy the scenery. Tomorrow is another day, but today isn't over yet."

Odd, thought Jill. She took the basket which seemed heavy for a sandwich and tea and headed down Main Street toward the park.

~

After Nick left Mountain Mama's he walked straight home. Past Allen's market, past the old church, passed the pizza parlour, passed several unique shops and a decent sized park. He really should have stopped at the market to replace the wasted grocery items that he had ruined. He just wanted to get home and put an end to this farce of a day. Anika, thankfully, said nothing on the walk home.

When he came to their house a couple of blocks past the park he turned to Anika.

"I'm sorry for the whole afternoon. I need some alone time to think so I am just going to play the piano for a while. I hope you don't mind. Here are the keys to the Jag and fifty bucks. Drive to Beckley if you want or just hang around town and try to meet up with kids from school. Maybe they hang around the pizza parlour."

"Really, dad?" She had a scowl on her face but she grabbed the keys and money and headed to the garage. He really should get her a car of her own. He was just too tired to think about what shape the Jag would return in. He would think about that tomorrow. He didn't even bother with food. He went straight to the piano and for the next forty-five minutes, he played from his heart and soul. He had always been able to see the music in his head, even when he was a little boy. And once he had played through a piece a few times, he could remember it. Then he would add his own special touch to it. It had always come to him naturally but as far as he knew, no one else in the family played the piano. No one besides Anika even had any musical talent. He had thought these things ran in families.

He was alive in his music and Anika said the same thing about her music on the violin. Like father, like daughter he supposed. He continued to let the music fill him as he felt his body and spirit unwind. The music always lifted him up to a place where he was at peace. Then his phone rang.

Who would be calling him now except Anika or someone connected with his building project. Neither call could be good. He answered the phone.

"Hi Mr. Wallace. This is Josie from Mountain Mama's. Sorry to bother you at home but Anika listed this number on her employment papers."

"It's okay," said Nick. "What can I do for you?"

"Well, I'm just calling to see if you or Anika have any food allergies or dietary restrictions for when you come to supper tomorrow. Wouldn't want to cause you any more trouble than we already have, now would we?" said Josie.

"No, we have no restrictions, but it was nice of you to ask," said Nick.

"Have you gotten any rest or food since you left the restaurant? We really should have offered to feed you before you left."

"Actually, I haven't eaten yet but I am trying to relax, and again, thanks for asking."

This is a strange conversation thought Nick. *Do all restaurants around here call their guests with these questions?* She was saying something else and he hadn't heard.

"What was that?" he asked.

"From your address on Anika's paperwork, you live in a nice area not too far from the park. I was just saying the park is a nice place to sit quietly and think. Not too much activity this time of evening and if you're real quiet, you may see some deer come out."

"Thanks for the tip. Anything else I can do for you?" Nick closed the cover on the piano keys.

"Nope. I think that'll do it," said Josie. She said her goodbyes and Nick hung up thinking how neighborly the people in this little town were. You sure wouldn't get that in New York City. But a walk in an outdoor setting did sound good and he passed a park just a couple of blocks before he reached his house.

He changed into khaki shorts and a black tee shirt and headed out the door. Maybe sitting among nature watching for deer would be a good way to end this day. Before he went home, he would stop at the market for something to eat. He was getting pretty hungry.

He headed into the park and noticed Josie was right. Not many people around. Just a young couple with their children on the swings. Other than that, no one. He headed for some pick-nick tables he could see farther into the park. He could stretch out on one of those and watch for birds.

He came to a sunny patch and bounded up the seat to sit on top of the table.

"Hey! Watch it!" A female voice spoke from nearby. "You nearly knocked me off the bench."

Nick looked around startled to see a woman sit up on the bench on the table's opposite side.

"I'm so sorry! said Nick. "I didn't see you there." He started to get down but she stopped him.

"Hi again," she said.

"I'm sorry, but have we met?" Now that he thought about it, her voice sounded familiar.

Jill looked at Nick for a full thirty seconds before she responded.

"It's really hard to say."

She stood up and came around the table. Nick was able to get a good look at her. She was tall and well built. Her clothes fit her curves very, very well. She had an extra fifteen pounds or so, but man! In all the right places! Her dark red hair was damp and un-styled, no makeup, and what beautiful eyes! He wasn't sure he had seen eyes that color before. He felt a spark of attraction which confused him. He was usually attracted to small, skinny blondes in designer clothes and five inch spiked heels. Or maybe that was what his mother's influence had led him to believe he was attracted to. Another thing to think about at another time. He didn't know what to think but he did know he wouldn't mind spending a few minutes in this woman's company.

"Hi, I'm Nick. I'm new around here." Nick extended his hand to her.

Jill took it and realized that Nick had no idea who she was. No recognition at all or that he had just spent the disastrous afternoon with her on her TV show. She cocked her head sideways still looking at him. She could have some fun with this!

"And you would be?" Nick continued and noticed he was still holding her hand.

"Happy to sit next to you on that pick-nick table." Jill gave his hand a lingering shake and a little squeeze before she let go.

She climbed to sit on the top and Nick followed. Jill scooted a little closer to him. He could smell her clean soap smell and something citrusy maybe? He wanted to put his nose in the crook of her neck and just breathe in her scent. Maybe even taste her neck with the tip of his tongue.

Down boy! What was he thinking!? Nick edged a little away, but he saw that she noticed.

"Are you okay? I didn't mean to get all up in your space dude." Jill leaned closer.

"Oh no," said Nick. "It's just that I have had an awful day and haven't eaten since breakfast. I think low blood sugar may be affecting my brain." As good an explanation as any, he guessed.

She smiled at him and it was all he could do not to reach over and kiss those soft, perfect lips. *There I go again* he thought. What was wrong with him. This was so out of character. Had it been that long since he had had a date or looked at a beautiful woman? He couldn't remember when he had ever been so attracted to any woman, much less one from the mountains of West Virginia. But something about her was familiar. He just couldn't put his finger on it.

Wow, thought Jill. She didn't think she had it in her to affect a man this way. He was showing signs of obvious attraction to her. Maybe it was the effect he was having on her as well or the fact that she knew he didn't recognize her that made her cast her inhibitions to the wind. Most men just saw her as too heavy or too West Virginia to take the time to really look at her. It was the skinny blondes that got all the attention.

"I'm sorry, what did you say your name was? You seem somewhat familiar." Nick looked closer.

"Did I mention that I have a basket full of food?" Jill sidestepped the question again. She silently wondered *why did she have a basket full of food*? She'd wager that Josie set this up.

"Food? That would be awesome!" Awesome? He never used that word. At least not since he was sixteen or so.

"I can't believe you just said awesome, dude," said Jill. "Are you still in high school?"

"No, but I have a teenage daughter and I think she may be rubbing off on me."

"Yeah, maybe," murmured Jill. She proceeded to set out the food as they both moved from the table top to the bench. Josie had done well. She had packed turkey salad on croissants, home- made sweet potato chips, and chocolate nut cookies. All Jill's recipes. She also found a couple bottles of sweet tea in the bottom of the basket.

"You have enough food for two. Were you expecting someone?" said Nick.

"Not really," said Jill. "My sister packed it. Maybe she was hoping someone would come along who needed a good meal."

"Well, she was right!" Nick's mouth was watering. "It all looks very tasty." But he was looking at Jill instead of the food.

He is so gorgeous, thought Jill. She didn't understand why he was looking at her that way. *No Jill* she thought. *You will not go down that road and risk losing the confidence you worked so hard to gain. Not today. Just enjoy it while it lasts, girl, because tomorrow when he finds out who you are, he won't give you a second glance.*

They proceeded to eat the meal and make small talk. He explained he was a single dad and would be living here for the next two years while he built a resort between Beckley and Fayetteville. The ground breaking would be in two weeks, so his family would be in town for that. *God help him*, he thought. He talked about his daughter and that he dabbled in playing the piano a bit. He wasn't about to tell her about his concert tours. Who knows? Maybe she had heard of him.

When he asked her what she did for a living she hesitated.

"Oh, this and that."

And to where she lived.

"Oh, around."

About the only thing he did learn was that she was, indeed, single.

They finished the meal and Jill put the leftovers back into the basket. She stood and brushed crumbs from her clothing and he did the same.

"That was the best food I have eaten in a long time," said Nick. "Did your sister make it?"

"As a matter of fact, it was made at Mountain Mama's restaurant," said Jill looking to gauge his reaction.

He looked surprised.

"I am so glad to hear that. My daughter and I are having dinner there tomorrow evening and to be honest, I was a little leery about what kind of food, or the quality, we might be served. I've met Mountain Mama and wasn't looking forward to eating her food."

Jill's only reaction was to narrow her eyes a bit before speaking.

"Mountain Mama is the best cook around. You have nothing to worry about. She'll do you right. As will the chef. And the owner."

"So, you know them all?" Nick figured in a small town, everyone knew everyone.

"Yes, I do and so, it sounds like, come tomorrow, so will you."

"I know this may sound strange since we just met, but I feel really comfortable around you. Since I don't know many people yet, I'd like to see you again." Nick felt he stumbled over his words.

"I think we'll meet again, maybe sooner than you think."

She wet her lips with her tongue and stepped closer to him. She bent over to pick up the basket and her shoulder grazed his chest. It felt like an electric jolt to Nick. She stood to her full height. Her face was about three inches from his.

"Until then."

Nick leaned in. He was sure she was going to kiss him but at the last minute, she turned and started to walk away. He couldn't take his eyes off her.

"Wait!" He called out to her. "How will I find you?"

She looked over her shoulder. "Don't worry dude, I'll find you."

As she walked away, Nick realized she hadn't answered a single question and the only person to ever call him 'dude' was Mountain Mama.

Six

A sense of unease fell on Nick as he walked up the stone sidewalk to enter Mountain Mama's restaurant. It was still a little before six in the evening and quite a few people were sitting on the front deck waiting for a table to open up that would accommodate their party.

That was a good sign thought Nick. He had done some asking around town today about the place and learned that people came from as far away as Charleston just to eat here. Their meeting rooms were booked out for weeks and the family provided entertainment if needed. He had learned that this was a family run business and everyone said there was no finer bunch of people in all of West Virginia as the Dennison family.

So why did he have goose bumps about crossing through the door? He had been thinking a lot last night about the girl from the park. Was he afraid he might run into her here? He would love to run into her again, but something bothered him about the way she called him 'dude'. He slowed his gait and Anika ran into him.

"You're lame, dad! I'm going to go find Josie and Matt." She took off up the stone path and went inside.

He was here to discuss the aftermath of yesterday's events, but his thoughts kept going back to that woman and her simplistic beauty. And his unexpected attraction to her. And the whole 'dude' thing. He couldn't get it out of his head. Anika was right. His 'lame' head. He had a bad feeling.

He took a deep breath and entered the restaurant where he was met by Lorraine. She led him up the stairs and into a small banquet room. He could see Anika and Matt seated at a large round table talking animatedly. Josie was talking to twin girls who seemed to be waitressing the room.

Jim came over to shake his hand and told him Jill would be down 'directly'. Lorraine left his side to tend to Nana who had just entered.

He saw the room was set up with two large round tables made of polished wood, and that each had five place settings. The twin girls were introduced to him by Josie as Marlene and Darlene, her cousins. They were very pretty as well as identical and looked to be in their early to mid-twenties. They each had short, dark hair and big blue eyes. They were small and reminded him of pixies. They showed him to a side table set up with pitchers of ice water and tea along with hot coffee and he helped himself to a glass of the ice water.

He was taking his second sip when he saw a woman enter the room. He started choking on the water and spilled some down the front of his designer shirt. It was the woman from the park! He was still coughing when she walked over to him. At closer range he wasn't so sure this *was* the same woman. Something was off. A close relative maybe? She was tall and dressed in a straight, black skirt a couple of inches above her knees, a green lacy shirt and black heels. Her hair was a dark reddish color with burgundy highlights but looking into her eyes made him doubt that this was the same woman. The woman's eyes were a vivid green.

Nick wasn't sure what to say. He wavered back and forth but couldn't seem to form any intelligent words. This must be the 'Jill' he kept hearing about, but was she the woman from the park? There were differences as well as similarities. Finally, his brain kicked in. He needed to focus on why he was there in the first place.

"I'm here to see the owner," said Nick.

"You're lookin' at her," said Jill.

Okay, thought Nick. "How about I speak to the chef."

"You're lookin' at her," said Jill with a straight face. He was afraid to ask the next question.

"How about Mountain Mama," said Nick dreading the answer.

"You're a lookin' at her!" Jill responded in Mountain Mama's raspy voice. "Hi, I'm Jill Dennison," and she held out her hand.

Nick just stared at her and she dropped her hand. She was Mountain Mama and he had called her a toothless old bat to her face! He was mortified! He had not realized that Mountain Mama was a character and not a real person. *So it was okay to call a real person a toothless old bat*? He'd have to have a serious look at his manners and intentions toward others.

"So, you're the owner, chef, and Mountain Mama who, as it turns out, is a character, and not a real person," said Nick summing it all up.

"Can't get nothin' by you, dude," said Jill.

Dude? He was trying to summon the courage to ask that last question.

"Did we meet in the park last evening and share sandwiches and tea?"

"Like I said, can't get nothin' past you," said Jill.

Nick realized he had been holding his breath and he slowly let it out. Jill stepped closer to him and they locked eyes.

"Gotcha!" Jill poked him in the chest with her finger.

Nick, stunned, stepped back. "You look different. Your eyes…"

"Are green today," said Jill just as Nana walked up. She gave Jill a big hug and addressed Nick.

"Ain't she a beauty? Purtiest gal in these here mountains. "Ere ye lookin' to court her or 'ere ye here to cut a rusty?" said Nana.

"What?" Nick was feeling really out of place.

Jill intervened. "Cut a rusty or cut a shine. Both are West Virginia for 'throw a fit' or 'cause a scene'. You should know all about that."

Jill got Nana a glass of water and seated her at the table, opposite Anika and Matt. Jim came over and greeted a young couple who were just arriving.

"Nick, I'd like you to meet my oldest son, Mark, and his wife, Nancy. They run the Mountain Mama's in Blacksburg, Virginia."

"So, you have more than one place," stated Nick. Jill came over and gave Mark a hug.

"Hey, little brother!" She hugged Nancy as well and patted her slightly rounded belly. "How are you feeling? Last I heard, you weren't supposed to travel. Is this okay with your doctor?"

"I'm past the first trimester and the morning sickness seems to have worn off so I can go where I want now," Nancy responded. "I am tired a lot, though."

Jim spoke to the group. "Everyone is here now so let's all have a seat and enjoy our supper."

Jill led Nick to a table and sat him between herself and Nana. Jim and Lorraine joined their table and Mark and Nancy sat with the younger group.

The twins began to bring in the food, family style, on large platters and sat them in the middle of each table along with a basket of corn muffins and a plate of butter. There was meat loaf, red skin mashed potatoes, green beans with bacon and a cucumber and onion salad. Nick's mouth started to water.

Jim stood. "Let's all bow our heads and I'll bless the food." He said a short prayer before the platters were passed around the table.

Nick felt overwhelmed. *This was what a real family should be like* he thought. He had never experienced this with his parents or siblings. The closest thing was when he and Anika lived with aunt Bess. When Nick was home, they all ate together at the table. Now they each ate separately, on their own schedule. She, mostly in her room or out.

Nick felt his eyes start to water and when he looked over at Anika, she was blinking her eyes hard as well.

Jill was watching Nick as they passed the food. He seemed to be having some emotional difficulty. Maybe she shouldn't have played him at the park. She really hoped she hadn't hurt him but on the other hand, she hoped he wasn't a wuss. Sometimes she could come on too strong and unintentionally 'put someone off,' as Nana would say.

"I hope being thrown in the middle of all of us Dennison's isn't too much for you, Nick," said Jill.

"I have to say I didn't realize there would be this many people having dinner but it seems whenever I enter the door to this place, I get thrown or pushed into something," he said with a smile. He locked eyes with Jill again and neither looked away.

"Supper," said Nana patting Nick's arm.

"Excuse me?" Nick pulled his eyes away from Jill's.

Nana continued. "Supper. That's what you're a eatin' here in this neck o' the woods. What do ye think o' my Jill's cookin' young man?" She continued without waiting for an answer. "Jill, ye know the way to a man's heart is through his stomach, so ye best be a feedin' this 'un up if you're a wantin' to keep him."

"Nana!" said Lorraine. "They just met, and not under the best of circumstances. You talk like that and he won't want to come here at all!"

"This food is excellent! I've never had meat loaf this good, and these corn muffins..." Nick said while wiping his mouth. "I think I could eat the whole basket!"

"We'll send some food home with you when you leave," said Lorraine.

"Do you all eat together like this often?" asked Nick.

"As often as possible," said Jim. "Mark and Nancy came in for our country band practice. That's something we do as much as we are able. The family band will play on Saturday and Sunday evenings this weekend. You should stop by and check us out."

"Do you all play?" asked Nick.

"All of us play at one time or another. Josie handles the entertainment side of Mountain Mama's. She puts together a monthly schedule depending on who is available. Mark comes when he can and most of us play multiple instruments so we can sit in for each other if we need to," said Jim.

"So, what do you play?' Nick asked Jill.

"Mostly I play the guitar and banjo. Some mandolin. Most of the time I play as Mountain Mama but not always. And I sing a little too. We all do," she amended.

"Sings like a canary, that 'un does," said Nana. "I used to play the pi-anny but ole Arthur got hold of my hands and I can't do it much now. I play the washboard sometimes though."

"Well, that's different. I don't think I have ever heard that played before," said Nick.

"Lorraine plays the piano now and Matt can cover for her if needed," said Jim. "I play the steel guitar and so does Mark. I also play the spoons and the jugs."

Nick was having a hard time picturing this in his mind having spent his life in concert halls playing classical music. He rarely ever listened to country music let alone a homemade country jug band. He doubted he'd missed much.

"Matt is the main fiddle player, though. You'd have to hear him play to believe it. I understand your Anika plays the fiddle too," said Lorraine.

Nick shouted. "My daughter does not play the fiddle!" Everyone stopped eating and turned to stare at Nick.

"Dad!" Anika shouted back at him.

"I told ye," said Nana. "He's a gonna cut a shine."

"She plays the violin!" clarified Nick.

"I knowed you was a Mr. High and Mighty," said Nana. "What's wrong with playin' the fiddle?"

"Nothing's wrong," stated Jill. "Nick is not used to our brand of entertainment. He's in for something of a culture shock, I'm afraid."

"I apologize," said Nick. "That was rude and uncalled for, but Anika is something of a virtuoso on the violin. She's been playing since she was five years old."

"Same with Matt," said Lorraine. "But he can play any instrument, not just the fiddle. Piano, guitar, drums, but he never really took to the harmonica though. That's Jim and Josie's thing." Lorraine continued. "The twins join us sometimes to sing and do a little clogging. Aunt Gladys and Uncle Frank join in as well. I don't think you've met them yet."

"I won't be able to stop in this weekend or next," said Nick. I'm building the new Grand Wallace Mountain Resort over near Fayetteville and the ground breaking is in two weeks. I'm already running behind. I want to get a good start on construction before winter sets in," said Nick. "I'll be with the contractors and architects making last minute changes and making arrangements for my family coming in for the ceremony."

"I've heard about that," said Jim. "It's supposed to be the largest resort in the state, and will bring a lot of jobs to the area. What a boost to the economy!"

"Wait," said Jill. "You wouldn't be connected to *the* Wallace's of the Grand Wallace Hotel chain, would you?"

"I'm afraid so," said Nick. "Andrew and Margaret Wallace are my parents."

"Wow! No wonder you were so upset about being called Alphonse Laurant. He's your signature chef in the Grand Wallace New York," stated Jill trying to stifle a laugh.

"Right, and he has a particular dislike for me," said Nick. "I caught him hitting on Anika and threatened him with jail if he ever came near her again."

"Don't ye be a gettin' so hot under the collar over some ol' codger after yer young 'un. Codgers has been after young 'uns since I was a young 'un myself," said Nana.

"Maybe so," said Jill. "But that doesn't make it right, Nana. And Alphonse Laurant is not an old codger. I've never met him, but I have heard he can be very difficult."

"That's putting it mildly," said Nick. "He's going to hit the roof when he hears of my fiasco. He's going to think I staged it to get back at him."

Jim relayed the conversation he'd had with Mr. Laurant's agent to Nick. "I sure won't say anything. Hopefully you're right and he'll never know about it."

Nick was debating about having another corn muffin when the twins started clearing the platters and announced they would be back with dessert. Nick wasn't sure he could eat another bite.

"I made a cranberry bread pudding and a walnut carrot cake."

"It's a good 'un," said Nana.

Nick noticed she really hadn't eaten very much. Mostly just moved the food around on her plate. Nick looked to Jill.

"I'll tell you later." Jill gave him a wink.

He was glad to hear there would be a 'later'. Nick had some of each dessert and wasn't sure he would be able to waddle out of there.

After the food was cleared away and some boxed up for Nick and Anika to take home, Jill spoke to her mother.

"I think you might need to take Nana home."

Nick noticed that Nana seemed to be dozing off at the table, so Lorraine started getting her mother around to take her home. She thanked Nick for coming to supper with the family and invited him back anytime for a meal 'on the house'.

Nana had developed a blank look on her face and Lorraine led her away talking softly to her. Jim shook Nick's hand and apologized again for the whole misunderstanding.

"I'm an attorney by trade so, hopefully, I can keep this from escalating if Alphonse does get wind of it."

"That would be greatly appreciated," said Nick. He shook hands with Mark and Nancy and watched the twins continue to clean up. He was left in the room with Matt, Anika, Josie and, of course, Jill.

"It's too bad you can't come by and hear some 'good ole country music.' We are going to be featuring our most requested songs." Jill started removing the tablecloths so they could be laundered.

Anika jumped up and asked if she could come and watch. Nick said that would be fine.

"Would you like a small demonstration?" Matt jumped up full of enthusiasm. How about it, Sis? I'll grab the banjo and guitar." Matt left the room followed by Anika.

"Hey! Grab my harmonica," yelled Josie. "Meet us on the back deck," she said to Jill and Nick as she followed the others.

"Well, Nick, what did you think of this big family gathering?" Jill was curious. "Did we scare you away?"

Nick considered the question. "I have a large family as well except I have never had a single dinner around a table with them. I was a little overwhelmed at first, but then I realized how much I have been missing. I really enjoyed it. Thank you for inviting us."

"It was the least, *and I mean the very least*, we could do considering what we did to you," said Jill emphatically.

"I'm over it as my daughter would say," replied Nick. "I'm sorry too, for 'cutting such a shine' as your Nana would say. I'm not usually that demonstrative but with this move, the project, and Anika punishing me for all of it, let's just say it's been stressful."

"A teenager definitely changes the dynamics in a household. I know Josie gave my parents a run for their money and the twins! You should talk to aunt Gladys sometime. She can tell you stories and give you advice like nobody else," said Jill.

"That was like my aunt Bess." Nick swallowed a couple of times and changed the subject. "How about a tour of your restaurant? It's quite the place."

"Okay," said Jill. "Follow me, man. I'll give you the fifty cent tour and then we can join the others out back."

Jill led him through the restaurant and it's main kitchen. She stopped to chat with some customers and kitchen staff. Nick met two of her Sous Chefs, Jean and Lance who were also cousins.

"Is there anyone that works here that is not a relative?" he asked.

"Sure. Of course. But there are a lot of us and we try to employ our own as much as possible. I do have a program to hire ex-cons who have had a hard time finding employment and also those with physical handicaps."

"I wish I could say the same for the Grand Wallace chains, but to be fair, I really don't know. We are not close in my family and rarely talk except to discuss business."

"That's sad," said Jill. "I don't know what I would do without my family. It's nice to know there is always someone there to watch your back, you know?"

"No, I really don't," said Nick. "Well, I sort of did when my aunt Bess was alive and I try to be there for Anika, but she makes it so hard."

"Are you lame, dude?" said Jill.

"Lame?" said Nick. "I'm the lamest!"

"Hey, the best defense is to go on the offense I always say," she said.

Nick stopped short.

"I'm sorry, did I say something wrong?" asked Jill.

Nick put a hand on each of her shoulders and looked into her eyes. "That's exactly what my aunt Bess used to say. I really, really needed to hear that right now. Thank you." Then he gave her a big hug. Hard. She was at a loss for words and that almost never happened. So she just stood there and let him hug her.

After a few more minutes she broke contact, even though it was the last thing she wanted.

"Let's head on out to the back porch to sit a spell." She continued the tour on the way. "You were in one of the small banquet rooms for supper and there is another the same size upstairs as well. There is also a large banquet room and my personal living quarters. I am the only one who lives on site."

"Wow," was all Nick could say.

She continued. "There is another medium sized banquet room downstairs and you have already seen the studio kitchen."

"Yes, I have," Nick said a little too sarcastically.

"Okay, lame dude, come on out back and listen to some real mountain music."

He could hear someone playing a harmonica and some kind of stringed instrument, maybe the banjo, but whoever it was, they were really good.

They emerged onto the back deck and Nick saw a beautiful mountain scene. The back yard had a large herb garden and some berry bushes that looked like blackberry and raspberry. Maybe even a strawberry patch. But the rise of the Blue Ridge mountain scene took his breath away. Even more beautiful than the one he could see off his back deck.

He turned his attention to those gathered around a small table talking and laughing. The deck had several small tables and a large stone fire place as well as a gas and a charcoal grill.

"Wow," Nick said again. The music had stopped when they came out and Jill could see Anika was going to insult her dad again, so Jill stepped in quickly.

"Anika, your dad is lame, so I brought him back to you."

She saw Anika's mouth shut.

"My dad's not lame." This shocked Nick because he heard this out of her mouth all the time.

"Sure he is. You said so yourself," said Jill.

"Well, he really isn't. In fact, he's…"

Nick quickly cut her off.

"He's wanting to hear some real mountain music!" He was sure she was going to point out that he was famous and he did not want to reveal that here.

"Okay Sis, how about some 'Dueling Banjos' and maybe follow that with 'Foggy Mountain Breakdown'" said Matt.

"Have a seat and enjoy our brand of country music," said Jill.

Anika took a seat next to her dad. Without a fight. How about that. With just a few words, Jill was a miracle worker.

She took a banjo and she and Matt started to play. They made a clean transition from one song to the next and Josie joined in on the harmonica.

After a while, Matt put down the guitar and started to play the violin, or fiddle as they called it. He had been impressed before, but on the fiddle, Matt was riveting. He had to admit, this boy was something else. He could make a living at this.

After a few more songs they ended the jam session. Nick and Anika stood to their feet and clapped heartily. Josie, Matt and Jill took an animated bow and joined them at the table.

"That was awesome, wasn't it dad?" Anika was speaking in a high-pitched squeal.

"Awesome," agreed Nick. "Matt, you can really play that violin and that banjo, and guitar too. And Josie, the harmonica, I'm speechless! And Jill, you are a banjo master."

"Get out of town, dude!" Jill was a little pink in the cheeks. "We've all been playing a long time but Matt really is a master. The violin will take him to Julliard next fall."

"Serious?" Anika was even more animated. "My dad went…"

Nick cut her off again. "Went by there on his way home once."

Anika gave him a look that said he was, once again, lame.

Nick cutting Anika off twice when she was about to say something important was not lost on Jill and as Nick and Anika took their leave for the evening, she was determined to find out what.

Seven

Later the next morning, Jill was in the studio kitchen preparing lunch for her family to eat before their practice session began. When they had family gatherings like this one, she usually fixed the food in the studio so that it did not interfere with the restaurant business end of things. Her mind kept wandering to Nick and his good natured personality. Not to mention his good looks and how he looked at her like she was something special.

I'm an overweight mountain girl and he is a model perfect New York aristocrat and he will never be really attracted to you, Jill thought to herself.

"Stop it! Stop it! Stop it!" Jill said out loud and then looked around quickly to make sure no one had heard her. "The Lord made me who I am and I should be proud of it. And I am proud of it and I will do my best to honor him in all I say and do," said Jill still out loud. *At least she would try,* she thought.

She was putting the finishing touches on the marinated vegetables she was serving. Her crock pot smoked sausage and cabbage stew with stuffed biscuits were just about perfect. She was checking the temperature of the food when her cell phone rang.

She put down the cheeseboard she was getting out of the cabinet for her cheese ball and answered it. It was her personal number so it would be one of her family members. Probably Mark, wanting to know what she was going to feed him.

"You've got her," said Jill into the phone.

"Hey, I didn't think it would be that easy," said Nick in his pleasant baritone. Jill nearly dropped her cheese ball as she was moving it from the fridge onto the board on the counter. Butterflies started up in her stomach.

"Nick, I wasn't expecting to hear your 'lame' voice on the other end of the phone asking if I'm easy!" She laughed and so did he. "To what do I owe this pleasure... or displeasure depending on the nature of this call?"

"Ouch," said Nick good naturedly. "It's a call for a couple of different reasons. One, to thank you again for such a nice time at your place last night. I don't know if I've ever had that much fun."

"Well, you have a daughter," said Jill. "So, somewhere along the way, there must have been some fun."

"Touche," said Nick. "But that's a long story for another time. The second reason I'm calling is about the ground breaking ceremony two weeks from today. My family will be here as well as the mayors from Beckley, Fayetteville, a couple of smaller towns and of course, Beaumont. Some reporters from local newspapers and couple of national news hounds and their cameramen will be on hand, etc., etc., etc. Anyway you get the picture and I'd like to invite them to a nice brunch. I was hoping I could book one of your banquet rooms. I do have a third question...would you like to attend the ceremony as well?"

Jill didn't respond right away and Nick took that to be a negative response so he continued.

"Your whole family is welcome too, of course."

"Sorry," said Jill. "It's just that when you started talking brunch, I started calculating space and menus. It's an occupational hazard."

"What I meant to say in a more eloquent way than I just did was that I would be honored if you and your family would join us."

"First, I can't speak for the rest of the family but I would love to come. The whole thing sounds so exciting! Hard work for sure, but I'm excited to hear more about it." Jill hesitated then continued.

"The only problem is that we are booked solid in all of our banquet rooms and it's doubtful that the restaurant would have enough room."

"Oh," said Nick very disappointed.

"Wait a minute, I'm still thinking here," said Jill. "I'm going to put you on speaker phone so I can take a pineapple cobbler out of the oven."

Nick's mouth started to water. Everything she cooked was unbelievably good. He wished he was there.

Jill explained, "I fix lunch for the family before practice."

Nick noticed the tinny sound of being on speaker and wondered if anyone else was present.

She continued. "I'm working in the studio kitchen."

"Hey!" They both said at the same time.

"Yes! Yes!" Jill became excited. "I'd be glad to open up the studio for the brunch. We'll set up tables and do the food prep right here." Jill didn't notice Nana enter and come to stand right behind her.

"That's great, Jill. Do I set things up with you or is there someone else who handles this sort of thing?" Nick spoke in a relieved manner.

"Hidy do there boy," yelled Nana. Jill nearly jumped out of her skin.

"Nana, you scared the britches off me!"

"Possum hockey girl. You're a talkin' to yer feller. I knowed he was after you the minute he set eyes on ye, I did."

Jill grabbed the phone and took it off speaker while Nana wandered off. "Nick, I'm so sorry. She has no filtering system. In her eyes, I'm a beauty and all men should be after me."

"You are a beauty and I wouldn't be surprised if all men weren't after you," said Nick sounding like he meant it. "I do have to ask though, is possum hockey something you'll be planning to serve or is that a West Virginia sport?"

Jill laughed and so did Nick. Jill hadn't been sure how to respond to his statement that she was beautiful so she was glad for the change in subject.

"Really though, possum hockey just means 'nonsense' or to quote myself, 'get outta town, dude.'"

"Okay," laughed Nick. "I have to get to work. Can you put together something for us and let me know the outcome and the cost? And, money is no object, really it isn't."

"Sure," said Jill. "My aunt Shirley will come up with a game plan and get back with you. She does most of the booking as well as bookkeeping around here."

"So what you're saying is that she is a bookie, right?" laughed Nick.

"Don't let her hear you say that. She's the director of our church choir! Nah! I'm going to tell her anyway," laughed Jill.

"Yeah, payback, I get it." Nick was still laughing. "See you in a couple of weeks then. I'll touch base with you to make sure everything is set a couple of days in advance if that's okay."

"Of course. See you later dude," and Jill hung up wondering if a man like him could really be interested in a girl like her.

Eight

The next couple of weeks flew past for Nick. He worked from daylight until dark everyday finalizing the ceremony plans, meeting with construction crews and sub-contractors. He wasn't having a lot of luck finding a place for his family to stay. That was proving to be a lot harder than he would have thought. There were no Grand Wallace hotels anywhere around. The nearest would be in Williamsburg, Virginia or Washington D.C. Both too far away. Most of the regular chains were booked up due to the up-coming Bridge Day, an annual celebration of the New River Gorge bridge in Fayetteville, West Virginia. People come from all over the United States to parachute off the bridge into the New River, white water raft, mountain climb, and browse the wares of authentic West Virginia craftsmen. Not to mention that this was the peak time in the fall for a color tour. The mountains were breathtaking with the reds, yellows, greens and oranges of the trees. This was exactly why he felt a resort would be profitable as well as a boost to the economy of the area.

If his family had been close or even some semblance of a real family, he would have invited them to stay with him and Anika. However, they were more like casual acquaintances or even strangers. He just didn't see any other option. *If* they would agree and that was a big *if*. Otherwise they would have to stay fifty miles away in

Charleston or in some 'hole' his mother would call it and he could not see anyone in his family agreeing to that. He could maybe persuade his siblings to stay with him but he was sure he could not tolerate his parents, but the likely hood of them agreeing to stay in the same house as he was slim to none. The slim being possibly to see Anika.

The ceremony was still two days away so he had better not put off calling them any longer. His parents would be the worst so he wanted to get that over with before he called anyone else. He phoned his parents pent house in New York and his mother answered.

"Hello mother," said Nick formally.

"Good evening. I assume you have a good reason for calling at this hour," she stated sharply.

Nick glanced at the clock to see it was only six o'clock. *Whatever*, he thought. "I'm calling to discuss arrangements for yours and father's accommodations for the ground breaking ceremony."

"So, you still plan on going ahead with this ridiculous idea to build a resort, bearing the Wallace name, in Hicksville, West Virginia? You know we won't give you a dime towards this heinous endeavor!"

"I know that, mother, and you know very well that I don't need your money. You know I have more money than I know what to do with. I could build two resorts with cash alone and still have more than anyone needs leftover." She made him feel like a little kid needing to stamp his foot for effect.

"Well, you must know that I won't lower myself to step one foot in that God forsaken state. Not if you put a gun to my head!" She stated this with as much force as she could muster.

Nick had to really work hard to rein in his tongue on that one and instead he asked to speak with his father.

"Your father won't be coming either!" she screamed.

Nick heard hushed voices and his father speaking.

"Give me that phone Margaret, and don't you dare speak for me again! We have had this discussion and we will have it again when I am finished on the phone!"

It sounded to Nick like the phone hit the floor or the wall. And then he heard his father's voice.

"Nick, how are you and how is my granddaughter?"

Huh? Interest in someone besides himself and sounding friendly too? *Something was definitely up*, thought Nick.

"We're fine, thank you for asking."

"Son, I will be down tomorrow and I've made my own hotel arrangements. I plan on trying to find an old acquaintance while I am in the area."

His father had an acquaintance in West Virginia? When had he ever been to West virginia? Calling him 'son'? He was starting to think maybe he had stepped into another dimension.

"Okay," he stretched out the word. "So do you require a car to meet you at the airport?"

"No, I'll be driving down in the Bentley."

Okay, he must have dialed the wrong number. His father never drove himself anywhere.

"Where will you be staying?" asked Nick.

"At a motel in a little town nearby call Meadow. I have to go. Your mother is getting ready to..."

Nick cut him off. "Cut a shine?"

"Yes!" His father laughed. "She's going to cut a big shine! I'll call you when I arrive," he said, hanging up.

Nick was astonished. His father seemed to understand the local lingo and he had never called him 'son' before. He spent a few minutes trying to reason it all out without any success. His mother was her usual lovely self, but his father? He would have

to think about it another time. He still had three siblings to call.

"Okay," he said out loud scratching his head, "On to the next one."

For the next thirty minutes he called his sister, Gwen, and his brothers, Rod, and Gerard. It went better than he would have thought. All were willing to stay at his house. They decided to arrive around noon on Friday, stay at his house on Friday and Saturday nights, and return to their homes on Sunday. They had not seen each other in a long time and even though he doubted any of them even considered that in their decision to stay more than one night, it seemed to be the social convention between them all. Rod would be driving down from Philadelphia, and Gwen and Gerard would be flying in to Charleston and renting cars.

Now that he had all that figured out he really should check in with Jill to make sure all was set for the brunch.

Then he remembered it was taping day and they would be winding down from that. So, he called Shirley instead.

Everything was set and the Dennison family would all be joining Nick at the ceremony. She and Gladys would stay behind and have everything set up for the brunch by eleven o'clock. Everything was all in place and Nick felt he could finally relax and spend some time at the piano.

~

Saturday morning Jill made sure everything was in order with her aunts, Shirley and Gladys. Shirley informed her that Nick had checked in as he said. They had everything ready to go and would be keeping an eye on Nana who would not be attending the ceremony.

The drive to the resort site was breathtaking and Jill could see why Nick chose this area. The fall colors were unrivaled anywhere else in the country. When they reached the site, they saw two or three local television stations represented and quite a few other official people as well.

Before Jill exited the car, she checked her appearance and once outside straightened her burgundy jacket and floral lace skirt. She joined her family in greeting Nick and Anika who gravitated over to Josie and Matt. Nick briefly introduced his brothers and sister to the Dennison family by first names only and then the ceremony got under way.

Each mayor, in turn, said a brief statement about the nature of the project and how it would impact their town.

The camera crew and the reporters moved in and out among the crowd.

Jill's mind started to wander and she noticed Nick's dad kept staring at her mom. Granted her mom still looked good for her age but she had not thought of her as a 'dude magnet' as Josie would say.

Now Nick's brother, Gerard, was most certainly a chick magnet. Maybe not in the same sense as Nick, but in an older, more mature way. His brother, Rod, was more of an introvert, she would guess, and had the look of a very serious bookworm with his slighter build and glasses. She took notice that none of the Wallace family seemed to interact with each other. Nick's sister, Gwen, was beautiful with her long, wavy brown hair and pleasant demeanor. She stuck close to Anika and fit in nicely with the younger group.

After the ceremony ended they all formed a road train back to Mountain Mama's. Jill rode back with her parents so that Gwen could ride with Anika and Josie.

"Mom, how about Nick's dad? He was sure checking you out!" said Jill.

"Stop it, Jill! I noticed that too and it was kind of creepy. There was something familiar about him though." Lorraine tapped her fingernails on the dashboard.

"I don't think he's ever been in West Virginia before but maybe you remind him of some big Broadway star." Jill continued to kid her mother.

Finally, her dad said, "something was very familiar about him too, but I just can't put my finger on it."

As Nick and his siblings followed the others to Mountain Mama's, his mind wandered back to yesterday evening after his brothers and sister arrived. Gerard came in first and enquired about Nick's concert tours and Nick explained he had cut back because of the project but had one scheduled with the New York Philharmonic in late October.

Gerard gave Nick a brief rundown of his life in Chicago, but nothing too personal, then he went to take a nap.

Rod arrived next and then Gwen about an hour later. Anika was glad to see her Aunt Gwen and the both of them had gone to the local pizza parlor and brought back pizza and subs for everyone.

They spent the evening barely interacting. Gwen and Anika spent time in her room with girl 'stuff' Nick figured. Rod had brought a book to read and Gerard worked on his lap top. If this had been Jill's family, it would have been a warm, loving good time. How he longed for that.

They all finally arrived and went into the studio section of Mountain Mama's. Jill was glad to see everything was set up and in order. The food was set up buffet style and had some breakfast as well as lunch fare combined. She could smell the chipped beef gravy and biscuits, quiches, bacon, sausage, and West Virginia ham. There was also fried chicken, broccoli casserole, potato salad, cole slaw, and hushpuppies and of course, a crock of pinto beans with bacon. Even some corn chowder. She had a separate area with desserts and drinks.

They all gathered around the mayor of Beaumont, Jack Hudson, who said a prayer for the food, the resort endeavor, as well as everyone in attendance. With that said, they all found seats and began a line to fill their plates. Jill sat at the table with her parents, Nick, Gerard, and Mr. Wallace. Rod and Gwen sat with the younger group and the officials all sat together.

The Wallace family didn't say much but seemed to be enjoying the food. Finally, Mr. Wallace looked at Lorraine.

"I can't seem to stop looking at you, Lorraine. I apologize, but I can't help thinking that we've met before."

"You look familiar to us too," said Jim.

"Have you been to New York lately, maybe to Marcel's?" Mr. Wallace continued to stare at Lorraine.

"No, we haven't been there," Jim laughed. "But we've heard a lot about it."

Mr. Wallace had barely glanced at Jim this whole time. He was too focused on Lorraine. "I'll think of it sooner or later. I always do."

"Well, I think it is doubtful," stated Gerard formally. "My family has never been in this state prior to today. My mother would never hear of it. No offense, but we prefer the city lights to the mountains and rivers. I manage the Grand Wallace Chicago and Rod manages the Grand Wallace Philadelphia."

He nodded to Jill. "Excellent brunch, may I say. Not my usual fare but delicious just the same. May I look around your establishment?"

"Of course," said Jill thinking how stuffy and rigid this guy seems. She wondered if he would be able to walk with that corn cob up his ass.

Lorraine interrupted her thoughts. "I'd better go check on Nana. She was still sleeping when we got back and I'm sure she's hungry by now." Lorraine got up and headed towards the stairs.

Mr. Wallace looked at Jim. "I stayed last night in a little town called Meadow. I thought I might try to look up an old acquaintance from my teenage years. Couldn't find any information, but what did I expect form something forty years ago."

Nick addressed Andrew. "Father, when were you *ever* in West Virginia?"

"Son, there's a lot you don't know about your mother and I and one day I will fill you in, but today isn't that day."

Lorraine came back leading Nana.

"My grandmother is from Meadow. Maybe she could be of some help," said Jill.

"Don't get your hopes up. Her memory isn't what it used to be," said Jim.

When Nana arrived at the table she stared at Andrew Wallace and he stared back. Nana started to cry.

"Andy Wallace? Is that you?"

Andrew stood to his feet with a shocked look on his face.

"Miss Lena?"

Then Jim stood up. "Andy? Andy Wallace? It can't be. I...I... didn't make the connection. It can't be!"

Andrew had tears streaming down his face. "Jimmy? I didn't catch your last name earlier. Jimmy Dennison? I came here looking for you! Miss Lena, I never expected... I was looking for the old boys home and was told it was torn down over fifteen years ago."

"Yes it was," said Nana. "I always wondered whatever happened to ye Andy after y'all got those poor girls away from that evil house down the holler. I prayed fer ye ever day since then." Then they all stood together and hugged for all the time they had missed.

Jill and Nick looked at each other. "Boy's home?" Nick was confused.

"My father spent three or four years in a boy's home in his teens over in Meadow. He met my mother there."

"In a boy's home?" Nick was even more confused.

"Sort of," said Jill. "Nana used to cook for the home and she lived in a small house behind the place. She raised my mom and aunts, Shirley and Gladys, there. My mom was the youngest."

"What would my father have had to do with that place?" wondered Nick out loud. "Granted, I really don't know the family background, but he's a New Yorker."

"There's certainly a story here," said Jill.

"My boys, my boys," cried Nana over and over. Lorraine had a shocked look on her face as well.

Andrew broke away. "Lorraine Marshall!" He grabbed her and gave her a big hug.

"Andy! I don't believe it! I'll go and get Shirley and Gladys!" She left at a fast trot and came back with her sisters.

Jill watched as Gladys and Shirley hugged Nick's dad as well. Nick looked like he was in a daze. He just kept shaking his head. Anika and Gwen came towards their table. Rod looked very confused and came to stand by Nick who had finally stood as well.

"I never would have believed it!" Andrew announced to the whole room. "I have been reunited with the most important people in my youth! My old friend Jimmy and Miss Lena, you made me the man I am today!"

So, they're to blame, thought Nick.

Andrew continued, "I know my son's and daughter don't understand but I promise, in time, I will explain it all. For now, let's just enjoy this time together." So Jim, Lorraine, Andrew, and Nana all moved closer together and were all talking at once.

"I'm very confused," said Nick. "I've never heard any of this before. How about you, Rod?"

"No," said Rod. "But it could explain a few oddities in my life." He and Nick looked at each other but were at a loss for words.

"I have a feeling you have a lot of secrets in your family," said Jill.

"I'm just finding that out myself," agreed Nick.

"And," said Jill, "I'll wager that some of those secrets rest with you, dude." She gave him a big wink and went over to help clear the buffet.

Nick and Rod were left with Gwen and Anika. "Dude?" said Rod and Gwen together.

Nine

By two o'clock that afternoon the room had been cleared and only the younger crowd remained. Jim and Lorraine had invited Andrew to stay with them overnight instead of at the small motel in Meadow. They all left but made plans to meet at Mountain Mama's the next morning for an early breakfast before church.

Nick said with a disgruntled sigh. "I'm sorry, but I don't attend church. You can count me out."

"Ah, dad! We used to go to church every Sunday with Aunt Bess. We were both raised in church! What is the matter with you?" Anika was whining.

"You know my feelings on the subject, and the subject is closed."

"You're lame dad and I'm going with or without you!" Anika continued to whine.

"Anika, you know I think you're really great, but you should have more respect for your dad. He's a good man and he loves you. Anyone can see that, but calling him 'lame' all the time is getting old," said Matt.

"Who died and made you boss?" Anika snipped at Matt, hands on hips and a scowl on her face.

Matt looked very irritated and his blue eyes were flashing. He looked away from Anika and said to the rest of the room, "I'm taking off now before I say something I'll regret!"

Josie stood up. "Good grief! You two have been inseparable for weeks now. You've become great friends, so what gives?"

"I'm just really tired from all the drama today," said Anika. "I'm sorry everyone. Grandfather threw us all for a loop. West Virginia has always been a taboo subject around my grandparents, so I don't understand any of this."

Nick was impressed that she took Matt's comments as well as she did. He was prepared for a hissy fit. Lord knows she had thrown enough at him. He was very impressed with Matt and felt he was a good influence on Anika. *Let's hope it lasts for a while*, he thought.

"Honey, I don't think any one of us understands this right now," said Jill standing to pull Anika closer. She put her arm around her in a comforting gesture.

"That's a major understatement," said Nick in response. "Rod, Gerard, has father *ever* called either of you 'son' before?"

"No!" Both said at the same time.

"Wait!" Jill looked around. "What's that clicking noise I keep hearing?" The others were looking around trying to hear.

"You know what I think? I think it's all those skeletons trying to get out of your closet!" Anika and Matt started to laugh. The others snickered a little too. All except Gerard.

"I'm sorry I missed the revelation earlier," said Gerard in that stuffy, arrogant way of his. "Our father would never stoop so low as to have had anything to do with a West Virginia boy's home. We don't usually associate with hillbillies." He had the grace to notice the others looking at him with shocked looks on their faces.

"No offense to those of you who have to live here."

"Gerard!" shouted Gwen. "I would think you would have had better manners than I've seen displayed while you have been here. Especially in the presence of our hostess!"

Must run in the family, thought Jill.

"I apologize for my brother," continued Gwen. "He sounds like he was raised in a barn!"

"No," said Gerard in that same manner. "I was raised by strangers in a boarding school in England which was most certainly better than being raised by mother and father. You all forget that I had to endure eight years of mother's forked tongue before I was sent away and believe me, I was ready to go! Frankly, I have had enough of all this and if I can get a flight, I am out of here *now!*" Gerard stalked out of the room.

"Land's of mercy," said Jill. "This is a surprise to all of us but I see what a shock it is to all of you guys. We all know mom and dad's story but not any of the other players."

She put her hand over Nick's and looked at each one in turn. She felt a little squeeze in return from Nick setting her heart beating double time.

"Once your dad explains it all to you, I'll be praying for you to be able to come to grips with everything."

"Like that'll help," snarled Nick.

"I'll go," said Rod quietly. "If the invitation to join you for church still stands, I'll go."

"I'm in too," said Gwen.

"I'm so excited! It'll be so much fun!" Josie was almost clapping her hands. "Aunt Shirley leads worship, mom plays the piano, and Matt plays the drums. Sometimes Jill sings specials, but not tomorrow."

Matt spoke up, "Anika, I'm sorry for being so ugly a few minutes ago. Forgive me?"

Anika pulled away from Jill and reached out to Matt. "You ugly? No way! Why you're the hottest..."

She stopped red faced realizing what she was about to say. "Ummm...I mean of course I forgive you."

Matt was as red in the face as Anika and Jill thought she had better intervene and pull the attention away from the kids.

"Hear that Josie? Our brother is hot!" Jill was being sassy. She was sure her sister would join in with her line of crap.

"Yeah. I hear that out on the street. He's a hottie all right!" Josie winked. "And speaking of hotties, Anika, your uncles are hot too. Ain't that right Jill?"

"Uhh...huh..." said Jill in a breathy voice as she stretched back in her chair.

"My uncles?" Anika scrunched up her face like she was smelling something foul. "No way! That's just wrong!"

"Josie, if you had to pick who would you say is the hottest?" Jill continued, leaning forward toward Josie now.

"Well, take Nick for example. He's really hot. Movie star hot. I'm not saying he's my pick for hottest but he's up there."

"My dad's not hot!" Anika almost shrieked. "That's just gross!"

"Oh I don't know," said Jill. "He looks hot to me." She winked at Nick.

"Then there's something to be said for Gerard. He's a little stuffy but I think the right woman could...hmmmm...'un-stuff' him a little. A hottie for sure."

"Hello. *You know we're sitting right here!*" Nick was waving his hand in front of them.

Josie continued without acknowledging the brothers. "Then there's Rod. I think I see hotness there too. You know what they say about strawberry blondes..." She let her speech trail off.

Rod perked up. "No, what do they say?"

"I think we can all agree that the Wallace brothers are hotness personified." Jill started to laugh. "I think that's enough said about that subject."

Nick was beet red and wanted to crawl under the table. Anika and Matt looked dumb founded. Rod was shyly looking at Josie.

"Well, now that that's settled, Anika, how about you and I go spend some time practicing, or anything else," said Matt in an uncomfortable fashion. He gave his sisters a 'what the heck?' kind of look. Matt took Anika's hand and they couldn't get out of the room fast enough.

Nick took a deep breath and shook his head to clear it. "Great," he said to the girls. "You know my daughter has a crush on your brother. That's the only reason she wants to work here and to go to church!"

"I thought so too, at first," said Jill looking pensive. She continued. "But she's a hard worker and Matt made it pretty clear up front that he was dedicated to his music and studies and had no interest in a romantic relationship."

"I think she took it pretty hard for a couple of days but it seems to have settled into a really sweet friendship," said Josie. "She comes over every day after school, they practice their fiddles…"

"Violins," interrupted Nick.

"Okay…violins," Josie continued. "Then they do their school work and if they are scheduled, they work their shift."

Nick felt a stab of fatherly guilt as he realized that he had no idea what Anika was up to these days. He was so busy at the resort site, that when he got home he crawled into bed most nights. When he got home at a reasonable time, she was out, so he spent his time at the piano.

Gwen came back in dragging Gerard behind her. "No flights until tomorrow afternoon, so Gerard will be joining us for church in the morning, isn't that right Gerard?"

"So *you* say." Gerard sat heavily on the chair and began to scroll through his phone messages.

He continued. "Nick and I in church. You'd better get out the hard hats."

"Hard hats?" asked Josie.

"Yeah," said Gwen, "because when the Wallace boys walk in, the walls will most likely come crashing down!"

"Cut it out," said Nick. "I never said I was going."

"No, *I* said you were going," stated Gerard in a matter of fact way.

Rod joined in. "You know, we have had *maybe* three conversations in our entire lives all in the same room. We hardly know each other, and the two of you are fighting. We should make an effort to at least try to get to know each other a little."

"Okay, time out dudes. Change of subject. How about we all go white water rafting tomorrow after church?" Jill looked hopeful. "We have a couple of family rafts. Josie's been a guide half her life and so has cousin, Lance. We could all fit in two rafts."

"Wait a minute. I plan on getting the heck out of here come tomorrow," said Gerard.

"I have to leave as well," said Gwen. "But it sounds like a lot of fun. I've never done anything like that in my life."

Nick piped up. "How about next weekend? It's Bridge Day!"

"What's Bridge Day?" asked Rod. Jill and Josie both launched into explanations about all the events and finally

Rod said, "I'm in. I'll fly down on Friday morning and stay with Nick." Then he hastily added, "of course, if it's all right with you and Anika."

"Me too, I'd love to come," said Gwen.

"Not on your life," said Gerard.

Stuffy old goat, thought Jill. *He really needs to get that corn cob out of his…*

Gwen interrupted. "I have to leave tomorrow to go sort out another situation with Alphonse Laurant. It's always something with him. Now he's threatening to quit and take his kitchen staff with him."

"I can tell you," said Nick, "the kitchen staff will not leave with him. But I think they *will* give him a standing ovation as he walks out the door."

"Just the same, I have to deal with him."

"What's his deal?" said Jill.

"He's too good a chef and too handsome for his own good. Women flock to him. It's disgusting to all of us who really know him."

"Do you have a picture of him or can you pull him up on your Smart Phone?" Jill interest had piqued. "I'd love to see the guy who is so much better than all of us mountain folk."

"Hey Gerard, make yourself useful and pull Alphonse up on your laptop," said Nick.

Gerard set his laptop on the table and typed in 'Alphonse Laurant'. Several sites popped up. He picked one and said, "there he is."

"In all his glory," said Nick. "Surrounded by his entourage, as he calls it. Self-satisfied idiot."

"What's that site there?" Rod was pointing at the screen. "It says 'Alphonse Laurant at Mountain Mama's Restaurant'.

Nick's stomach hit the floor. He heard Jill gasp and they gaped at each other.

"No way," they said in unison.

Gerard clicked on the site and the Wallaces all looked over his shoulder at the screen. Nick was horrified!

"Oh no!" Jill groaned. "Someone must have filmed part of the show with a phone and sent it to this site."

"I hadn't considered that," said Nick.

It was showing the part of the show where Mountain Mama was accusing Nick of flirting with her and then jumped to where Nick, explaining in his fake French accent to Lorraine, how he would prepare his non-edible food.

A fair portion of the show was there. To be fair, they'd had more phone calls asking when 'Alphonse' would join the show again than any other guest. Of course, she had not mentioned this to Nick yet. All of a sudden Rod and Gerard started to laugh. They were laughing and slapping the table until they had tears streaming down their faces.

"Uh oh," said Jill. "There goes that corn cob!" Josie kicked her under the table.

"Ouch!" said Jill.

"What is this?" laughed Gwen. "And who is that old bat?"

"What is it with you people and the 'old bat' label. Is that a family thing?" She explained that she was Mountain Mama and she gave them a run-down of what happens on her show.

Josie told them all about the mix up with Lorraine thinking Nick was Alphonse Laurant. This started Rod and Gerard howling with laughter all over again.

"Nick, I've got to say. I didn't know you had it in you," said Rod.

"I'm impressed," said Gerard still laughing.

"Cut it out," said Nick. "None of you are funny!"

"Apparently not. It looks like you're the only comedian in the family," said Gwen in her dry sense of humor. The guys laughed harder.

"Come on," said Nick, "If he sees this, I'm dead meat!"

"It's just a matter of time, dude," said Jill. "We'd better give dad a heads up. He may have to run damage control sooner than expected."

She explained to the Wallaces that her dad was a lawyer by trade and had already spoken with Mr. Laurant's agent.

Gerard also explained that he, too, was a lawyer and was used to handling legal aspects of the Grand Wallace hotel chain. He grudgingly agreed to speak with Jim about the matter.

Josie left to place the call to her dad and was followed by Rod. Gwen left to take another look around the restaurant taking Gerard with her, leaving Nick and Jill by themselves.

"We *so* don't need this right now," said Nick. "I'm going to have to pay *big time* for this."

"I know what you mean. I hate to say it but I bet this goes viral," said Jill.

"Wouldn't surprise me *at all*," replied Nick.

"How about we just wait and see. Maybe he still won't see it," said Jill.

"We can only hope," said Nick.

"And pray," said Jill. She took Nick's hand and said an earnest prayer.

"*Lord, I know you see the bigger picture in all this. I ask if it be your will, you would stop this from causing damage to the Wallace family and to us, here, at Mountain Mama's. I ask that you would strengthen those that need strengthening, and soften those hearts that need softening. And I ask that you would turn all of this around for good. In Your Son's name, Amen.*"

Nick squeezed her hand and could think of nothing to say except, "Amen," as well, and as he did, he brought Jill's hand up to his lips and kissed it.

They were just staring at each other. Jill's heart had stalled and she was afraid if he let go of her hand, it would never start again. She was falling for Nick.

No, I can't. Sooner or later he will realize I am too country for him and dump me, just like Geoffrey Beam, the third. She was not willing to go down that road again. It was just too painful.

Just then Josie came bouncing into the room because that's what Josie did, bounce.

"I have dad on the phone. He just heard from Mr. Laurant's agent. He saw the site and says Alphonse saw it too. He's threatening to sue."

Jill took the phone. "What do we do now, dad?"

"His agent, Victor DeVille, will try to smooth things over on his end and try to keep Alphonse from going to his lawyer. Andy says he will have some leverage because Alphonse is teetering on the edge of being fired anyway."

Jill put the phone on speaker and thought, *Victor DeVille? Sounds more like a male stripper than an agent.* They could hear Andrew laughing in the background obviously watching the site.

"He deserves this, you know!" Andrew yelled so they could hear.

Then Nick and Jill started to laugh as well. In her heart Jill knew God had a hand in all of this and she was looking forward to seeing how he chose to work it all out.

Ten

The following Friday dawned absolutely beautiful. Perfect weather for the start of the Bridge Day celebration. To Jill, there was not much that was more moving than a Blue Ridge Mountain sunrise. She had been up early to start the day's baking and getting in some extra time with her Bible and quiet time with the Lord. She was feeling pretty good. She had not heard anything else from Alphonse Laurant's agent. She knew her dad and Gerard had talked extensively with him on the phone and when Gerard left after church last Sunday, he had planned to fly straight to New York for a meeting with both Alphonse and Victor DeVille.

She hadn't heard anything this week from Nick either, but she knew how busy he was. She had been very busy as well, but her thoughts always seemed to go right back to Nick. She wasn't worried. She knew she would be hearing something soon about the weekend plans. Rod and Gwen were arriving at the Beckley airport today and Josie was meeting them. She would take them to Nick's place to let them settle in before a get together at her parent's home later in the evening.

Mr. Wallace had remained at the Dennison home all week and they, along with Nana, had been spending time over in Meadow reminiscing about the old days. This seemed to put a spark in Nana's memory and for that, Jill was grateful.

She was working in the studio kitchen later in the day trying to perfect a new recipe that would go on the holiday menu a few weeks before Thanksgiving. The phone rang and she checked the caller ID before answering.

"Hey girlfriend, what's up?" said Jill.

Her best friend, Brenda Montgomery, came back with, "same old, same old." Then after a short pause continued.

"Say, I heard you were hanging around with that new developer in town, what's his name? Rick something? Spill it. Come on. I want details!"

"It's Nick, and there are no details to give," Jill replied and then filled Brenda in on all the things that had happened over the last several weeks.

"Girl, I gotta look that site up!"

"Everyone else has, so knock yourself out," said Jill in a dry tone of voice. "How's Bonnie doing out in Chicago? Was she able to find a job?"

"Get this, my sisters have always been go-getters, you know that I'm sure, but Bonnie found a gig with a band in some respectable night club in the middle of downtown Chicago. She loves it and she is making *decent money*. And Georgia, she's singing three or four nights a week in a piano bar in the artsy part of New York. I forget the name. We still sing together at times but not as often as we used to."

"Yeah," said Jill, "I saw 'The Montgomery Triplets' on our schedule in December. I can't wait to see you all together again! So, what are you up to this weekend?"

Jill went on to explain that hers and Nick's family were planning to go to Bridge Day and also do some white-water rafting.

"We're planning to meet at my folk's house later this evening for a cookout. If you're not busy, why don't you join us? You can meet everybody. Come on girlfriend, it'll be a blast!"

"If you think I won't be intruding, I'd love to come," said Brenda. "Are you cooking?"

"Heck, no!" said Jill. "Mom and Nana have this one covered. Anyway, I've got to go so I'll see you later, about six o'clock."

"Sounds great," and Brenda rang off.

Nick was winding things up at the job site and handing the reins over for the weekend to his second in command, Dale Gentry. Nick felt bad that Dale would miss Bridge Day but a sprain to his left wrist would keep him from parachuting off the New River Gorge bridge as was his custom. He told Nick if he couldn't jump, then he didn't want to watch anyone else.

"I guess you will miss your morning weight lifting sessions too," said Nick as he stepped away from his drafting table.

"Well the doc did say not to lift anything over my head that weighs more than a hundred pounds," replied Dale flexing his huge biceps.

"What a shame," said Nick rolling his eyes. "I think we've covered everything and you know you can reach me by cell if anything comes up."

"I've got this. I have you on speed dial. Go enjoy getting to know you brothers and sister."

"Okay, I'm out of here," and Nick started up the hill to his Jag.

Dale yelled after him, "You really should get a truck or at least a four wheel drive. You're going to need it when winter sets in. I mean, the Jags great for getting chicks but not out here at this building site."

"I know, it's on my 'to do' list," and he climbed in the Jag and eased it the rest of the way up the hill to the road.

~

By the time he went home, showered, and changed it was time to drive to the Dennison's home out on Turkey Run road. He wondered where Anika was and how she would get all the way out there, but he knew she was resourceful and had probably already found a way.

He turned into the driveway when prompted by his GPS and followed a lengthy gravel drive winding up to a beautiful, three-story, renovated farmhouse on quite a bit of land. White with dark green shutters and a wrap-around porch, it was so inviting, he felt like he had arrived home. He could see a couple of white wooden benches placed in the yard and even an old tire swing suspended from a huge oak tree. Somewhere in the distance he could hear horses and what might even be a donkey.

As he continued to pull forward down the driveway, he could see ducks scattering out of the way. As he approached the front of the house, he could see several vehicles parked off to the side. And sure enough, there was Anika sitting in a front yard swing with Matt looking over some music.

He yelled to Anika. "Hey! How did you get here?"

"Matt picked me up as usual, but if I had my own car, he wouldn't have to."

"Ahhh… but then you would miss out on all this time with him," said Nick messing with her.

"Just give him some gas money. I'm sure he doesn't mind toting you around." Both their jaws dropped when Nick threw two, hundred dollar bills to her.

"Sir," said Matt cautiously. "I don't need your money. It's a pleasure to drive Anika around."

"I'm just kidding. Keep the money though, and Anika, we'll talk seriously about getting you your own car soon."

Nick continued up the porch steps and into the house. It looked like he was the last to arrive and most of the guests were on the back deck talking and laughing.

He could see Lorraine and the Aunts sitting at a table with a man he had not met, looking at some pictures. Rod and Gwen were in the kitchen with Josie and he could see Jill talking to a very pretty woman that he, also, had yet to meet. She saw him and pulled him outside into the crowd.

"I'd like you to meet my best friend, Brenda Montgomery. Brenda, this is Nick Wallace of the famed 'Grand Wallace' hotel chain."

"Howdy, Nick," said Brenda. "It's great to finally meet you but, you know, I'll be seeing you soon anyway at the parent teacher conferences next week."

When Nick looked confused, she continued. "I'm Anika's music history teacher up at the high school."

"I'm sorry, Anika has yet to inform me of this, as usual. Of course, I'll be there, and it's nice to meet you as well," said Nick.

"Something about you is really familiar," said Brenda as she continued to scrutinize him. "I know you from somewhere."

"Well, have you been to New York, maybe to Marcel's restaurant in the Grand Wallace New York?"

Nick was trying to throw her off base. With her being a music history teacher, he was sure she knew of his work and had probably been to his concerts. Maybe even owned some of his CDs.

"Yes. I have been to Marcel's, last year. My sister works in New York and we met there," said Brenda.

"That must be it then," said Nick. "I was in and out of there a lot and I spent time talking to the customers, so we probably did meet."

"Right, then it's good to meet you again," she continued but kept eyeing him like she just wasn't convinced.

"Son, son!" His father called him from across the deck. "Come over here and meet Frank Arlow, Gladys' husband. He's the pastry chef at Mountain Mama's."

Nick shook his hand and they exchanged pleasantries. He had learned last weekend that Aunt Shirley was a widow and the mother of Lance and Jean King, two of the Sous Chefs at the restaurant.

Nick had never seen his father like this. He was dressed in jeans and a flannel shirt and was laughing and having a great time.

"Father, may I speak with you?" Nick pulled him to the side. "How long are you planning on staying here?"

"Why son? Am I cramping your style?" His father laughed and slapped him hard on the back causing Nick to stumble a couple of steps.

Nick took a deep breath and tried again. "Father, how is mother taking all this with you staying here?"

"She's livid, just livid! I told her I am staying as long as I feel like and she will just have to deal with it. I may even buy a place here," said Andrew.

"Really, father, what is going on?"

"Nick, I have found a part of my life that I thought was lost forever. I can't lose that ever again. I'm getting the chance to really connect with my children, something I was never able to do while you were growing up. To me, that is precious and worth everything your mother will try to put me through. And in the long run, this will help your mother as well. I know you don't understand, but we *will* sit down and I *will* explain everything soon. *I promise.* For tonight, let's just enjoy the fellowship and good food okay?" Andrew slapped Nick on the back again and his tea sloshed all over Nick's clothing.

"Sorry son! Here's a towel." He started wiping the liquid off Nick.

"We have a surprise for after dinner. I mean supper." With that, he went back to the grill to join Jim and Frank.

Nick went back to join Jill and Brenda. "I don't think he plans to leave anytime soon."

"He looks like he fits right in," said Brenda.

Andrew and Jim were at the grill brushing sauce over the chicken and ribs.

"Let's get the rest of the food out here," said Jill. "The meat will be done in a jiffy."

They all pitched in to bring the food out to the buffet table on the deck and Aunt Gladys put the finishing touches on dessert, a blackberry buckle. Aunt Shirley and Lance were making homemade peach ice cream with peaches from the trees in the back forty. When the food was all set up and the guests ready to eat, it was Andrew who said the blessing. Nick caught Rod's and Gwen's eyes and Gwen gave a slight shrug and Rod just shook his head.

The conversation and good eating went on for over an hour. Nick was glad to see Anika eating more than a few bites. She always claimed to be on a diet so she could fit into the most stylish clothing. He thought Jill had been a good influence with her beautiful clothing and outlook despite not being a size two. She had joined the younger group's table and was looking at something Anika was writing on a napkin.

Nana was unusually subdued but no one seemed to pay much attention to her. Nick noticed Gwen was in a deep conversation with Lance and Brenda and thought this was a good time to step away from the table for a few minutes.

He had eaten so much and didn't want everyone to hear if he had to burp. He really should have stuck with the tea instead of all the pop he drank. He went into the kitchen and was glad he did. His burp turned into a loud belch. When he turned around to return to the deck, he ran right into Nana who had been standing behind him. He could feel the heat creep up his face.

"Did ye come in here by yer self to break wind?" she asked.

"Break wind?" Nick parroted.

"Ye know what I'm a meanin', break wind!" Then she loudly passed gas. The odor was foul.

Just then Jill came in. He saw her wrinkle her nose and pause for a few seconds before going to Nana.

"There you are Nana! No one saw you leave. Don't scare us like that!"

"I just came in here to break wind and found yer feller in here a breakin' wind too," she said pointing Nick out.

"Nana!" cried Jill.

"I just burped and then Nana came in..." started Nick.

"Sure Nick. Better out than in I always say." She led Nana into the living room and seated her in a comfortable chair.

Nick was mortified! Jill was never going to believe he wasn't farting in the kitchen. Jill passed him on her way back outside and took great pains to point out the way to the bathroom. He started to protest but realized the more he tried to explain, the guiltier he would look.

When the clean-up was done, Nick took a seat in the spacious living room as far away from Nana as he could get. Jill perched herself on the arm of the chair he was sitting in.

When they were all seated, Jim stood up and announced his old teenage band would play a few songs.

"Back when we were at the boy's home, Andy and I would get together with the girls and Miss Lena. We would play and sing for hours. We'll do a few songs for you. Bear with us though, it's been forty some years. In the old days Nana played the piano, but we'll let her rest tonight and Lorraine will play instead."

Lorraine took her place at the upright piano in the corner and to the Wallace family's surprise, Andrew picked up a guitar. Jim picked up one as well and the Aunts joined around and they began their rendition of 'Daddy Sang Bass'. Jim sang the main part but when they got to the chorus it was Andrew who sang in a deep bass voice "daddy sang bass" and Lorraine followed with "mama sang tenor", then the others all joined in singing in harmony.

Nick and Rod were astounded, Gwen, not so much. *Could things get any stranger*? thought Nick.

When the singing was over, the older folks sat around talking and drinking coffee. Nick pulled Gwen aside.

"You didn't seem all that surprised when father was singing and playing guitar."

"Not really," replied Gwen. "Sometimes when mother would have one of her meltdowns I would hear father singing and playing the guitar while she cried."

"I never knew that," said Nick.

"Well, now you do," said Gwen and she left to join Lance and Brenda on the deck.

Josie took Nana to get her ready for bed and Nick was standing in the kitchen alone when Jill came back in.

"Standing alone in the kitchen again, I see," she said. Nick started to protest when she gave him a big wink. She took his hand and pulled him out of the house and down the front porch to the swing in the yard.

"I hope you don't mind sitting out here with me for a while." Jill pulled him down to sit in the swing and together they got the swing in motion.

He looked at her and attraction kicked him in the gut. She was so beautiful with her long legs and sexy smile. He would never be able to look at another skinny blonde. He was done. All in. No one, but, no one had ever affected him in this way.

"I would love nothing better than to sit here with you for the rest of my life…I mean night," he quickly corrected.

She put her finger on his lips.

"Shhh. Just sit still and listen to the quiet."

Nick sat still and closed his eyes. He could hear crickets, lots of cicadas, and frogs he thought. He was even thinking he had heard an owl a couple of times. After a while he spoke.

"You know, it really isn't all that quiet out here. I can hear a lot. It's even quite noisy when you think about it. Just different sounds from what I'm used to in New York. It's more like growing up at Aunt Bess's place." It filled him with peace and a longing that he was just beginning to understand.

Jill was afraid to speak. Her palms were sweating. Then they heard a loud shriek, and another. Over and over it went. Nick jumped up thinking someone was being strangled to death. Jill started to laugh.

"Nick, come sit back down! It's just Nana's peacocks!"

Nick sat back down. "That nearly gave me a heart attack! I was sure someone was being murdered in the back yard!"

He took Jill's hand. He noticed goose bumps on her arms so he put his arm around her.

"I hope you don't mind. I'll save you from the peacocks," he whispered in her ear.

"The way it went, it looked like I would have had to save you," she whispered. Their faces were so close they could feel each other's breath.

Nick took a chance and leaned in. He slowly lowered his lips to hers in the sweetest kiss she had ever had. They pulled apart and locked eyes and at the same time came together again in hunger and passion. Nick deepened the kiss and it seemed to go on for hours until she realized she was almost sitting on his lap. She was kissing him all over his face and his hands were buried in her thick hair. Her jacket was off and so was one of Nick's shoes.

Then they both heard it.

"Well, well, well, sis. It's about time!" Josie, of course.

Jill moved into the seat again and started to straighten her hair when she noticed it was not only Josie, but Rod, Gwen, and Brenda as well. And coming out of the house was Matt and Anika. Nick coughed a couple of times to cover his nervousness and Jill started to clear her throat.

"I guess it's time to go," said Nick as he put on his shoe.

"Bedtime, for sure," said Brenda which got her a scathing look from Jill.

Thankfully, Matt and Anika hadn't noticed a thing.

"Good night Jill," said Nick. Then he leaned in so only she could hear and said into her ear, "I hope you have sweet dreams. I know I will."

He and the others left, leaving Jill watching Nick drive away wondering if her heart would ever be the same.

Marianne Waddill Wieland

Eleven

Saturday morning was as beautiful as the day before. Nick bounded down the stairs texting Jill that they would be there in a few minutes. He had packed a duffle bag with extra clothing just in case he fell in the river during the rafting trip.

Anika was in the kitchen sitting at the island eating cereal and didn't even look up when he came in. He noticed that she didn't have any of her usual heavy makeup on. Her face was 'clean as a whistle' as Nana would say.

"Hey! I haven't seen that pretty face in oh... for-ev-er," he stretched the word out kidding around with her. "No mascara, no lipstick..."

Anika interrupted him. "I see you wiped your lipstick off too."

Nick was confused. "What do you mean?"

"You had lipstick all over your face and the front of your shirt last night," she answered.

She still had not looked up at him. How did he explain this turn of events? She was bound to be upset.

"Listen Anika, I'm so sorry you had to see that and I know you must be upset, but Jill and I have become very good friends. I'm not sure how to explain…"

"No need, dad. There's been a bet going on to see how long it would take for you and Jill to get together."

Nick was aghast! "Really? You were taking bets? Who was in on it?"

"Everyone, Dad."

"Meaning?" Nick continued refusing to let it drop.

"The Dennison's, Uncle Rod and Aunt Gwen, the kitchen staff, the filming crew, the mailman…" she let her voice trail off.

"Alright! Alright! I get the picture! You can stop now."

"Grandpa won."

"He did not!" Nick was shocked.

"Oh yes he did and he's letting everyone know it too!"

"Great," said Nick. "Anika, are you upset?"

"No dad. Not at all. I think it would be great if you and Jill got married. I always wanted a mother, or step mother, or some kind of mother." She paused thinking. "I have grandmother and she is definitely a mother…"

"Anika!" Nick shouted. "Watch your mouth!" Nick tipped her face up to look her in the eye and smiled. "But you're right on that count. And Jill and I are not getting married. We barely know each other, but if you're okay with it, I would like to ask her out."

Anika looked up at him. "Jill and I have become close, Dad. I love Jill. I love all the Dennison's. But the next time you make out with her, which is really gross seeing your dad make out, by the way. I may be scarred for life!" She continued.

"As I was saying, the next time, just take her up to Snuggler's Point in the Jag like Matt and I do."

"What?!" Nick umped up with his hands balled into fists. "I thought you two were just friends?"

"Cool it, Dad! I'm just trying to get your goat. Matt and I *are* just friends. I've painfully had to accept that, and yes, everyone was watching out the front windows."

Nick wished he could be calm and nonchalant like Gerard in these kinds of situations, but his face reddened at the drop of a hat.

"How embarrassing!"

He texted Jill and she answered. "Gear up! There was a bet. Andy won. Maybe we should talk, not raft."

"Sounds like a plan," he texted back and they headed out the door to meet the others at Mountain Mama's.

Parking their cars proved to be difficult even though they had arrived early. Josie and Lance had each driven trucks with a raft in the back. After some general sightseeing, those planning to raft would head out to the starting point on the New River for a four-hour trip that would end close to the Dennison's home.

Once again, most of the Dennison's were there for the festivities. Nick couldn't help but compare this to his own up-bringing. Aunt Bess had made a good life for he and Anika. Despite the fact that she and his mother had come from lots of 'old money', aunt Bess had made life simple and pleasant. She had helped them both tap into their gifts and talents and given them the greatest gift of all. She had made sure Jesus Christ was at the center of their family. There had been none of that in his parent's home.

After aunt Bess was gone and he had moved back to the penthouse, he had lost all faith. He couldn't understand how a loving God could have let aunt Bess die like she had. And how could He have left Nick no option but to leave Anika with selfish grandparents that had never wanted her in the first

Place? Never even wanted any of their own children. The best that he could figure, they must all have been accidents. He had struggled with these questions for years and still had no answers other than a loving, caring God wouldn't.

The Dennison family was everything a real family should be in Nick's eyes and he could see how their faith in a loving God brought them closer together. *So how was his father fitting in so well*? It just didn't make any sense. Aunt Bess would tell him to have a little faith. Things were not always as they seemed on the surface and he was starting to think she may be right. *Lord, if you can hear me, help me to find my way and help me to guide Anika along her path. Oh, and if it isn't too much trouble, help Jill to want a future with us too.*

That was the first time he had prayed in years. He wanted that closeness the Dennison's had in a family of his own. A wife and maybe more children. He was only thirty two, so surely he could manage that.

He looked at Jill and she was so adorable with her Mexican print blouse gathered at the waist. She had paired it with skinny jeans and stylish hiking boots. Her hair was wavy today with lighter, amber streaks and her eyes were a light gray.

"Your eyes always seem to match your clothing," said Nick stating the obvious. "What color are they really?"

"These are the real things today. I have clear contacts in. I can wear many shades of contacts because of the light color of my eyes. I also have several shades of washable hair color that I just brush on. It helps me to feel a little different from just plain old Jill," she said shyly.

"Jill, you are a natural beauty. Enhancement is fine, but you really don't need it."

"Thank you, Nick. That is probably the nicest thing that anyone has ever said to me," she replied.

"How about you and me breaking away from the others for a while and spend some quality time on our own. I think we have some major talking to do," said Nick.

"You're right," agreed Jill. "A lot needs to be said before we move ahead with this … relationship? …friendship? What would you call it?"

"Let's get away and find out," said Nick with a smile on his face.

Lorraine, Nana, and the aunts were browsing the crafts and Nana was giving the vendors a hard time, as usual. Jill let her mother know that she and Nick were going their own way for a while and her mother promised to let the others know that they would not be joining the rafting trip.

They headed away from the main drag and towards the wooded area. "It would be great to get down near the river," said Nick.

"The only way to get down there today, other than to drive, is to rappel down the cliff or take the zip line," explained Jill.

"Oh...I don't know," said Nick imagining losing a finger in either activity.

"Come on, dude, don't be a wuss! It's a lot of fun! Let's take the zip line. You'll love it, I promise you'll be safe," she teased him.

He heard her mutter to herself, "those skeletons are clicking away".

They took the zip line to the bottom of the gorge and Nick had to agree, it had been a lot of fun.

"What a rush! Wow! I could do that over and over!" Nick was trying to catch his breath. He could see that Jill was a little breathless as well.

"Good. I'm glad you enjoyed it. I was afraid if you hadn't, the rest of the day may not go so well," she said looking sheepishly at him.

"I'm not like that, Jill. I wish I could erase the fit I threw the first day I met you. I can't really give you a good explanation for it."

"Don't sweat it, dude. Let's go find a quiet place to talk."

They walked along the river for about a quarter mile and found a good sized out cropping of flat rocks over the edge of the river. From there, they could watch the white water rafters race by. This area was probably a class three or four, Jill explained to Nick.

After they were seated and had waved to several rafters, they turned to a more serious discussion.

"Jill," began Nick. "I have dated a fair amount of women over the last several years, but I haven't had any serious relationships."

"You must have had one," said Jill. "Anika is proof of that. Where is her mother anyway?"

"On Broadway," said Nick. "She's a dancer and an actress. After giving birth to Anika, she never saw nor asked about her again. My family paid her not to abort Anika."

"How awful! What kind of person does that," cried Jill.

"A child," said Nick. "She was only seventeen when she became pregnant. I was only sixteen. We were both just children ourselves. Jill, I am only thirty two years old now."

"Wow," said Jill. "But you must have loved her, right?"

"Of course I thought so, but it was just raging, teenage hormones. Aunt Bess was a dance instructor and Erica was in a more advanced class than I was."

"Wait," said Jill. "You took dance lessons? Don't tell me, let me guess. Tap dancing...am I right?"

"And ballroom," said Nick.

"I *knew* it," said Jill. "The way you tried to imitate Mountain Mama. I told mom and dad that you looked like you were tap dancing."

"Anyway, to get back to the story, a male was needed in the advanced class for a dance competition and I was pretty good. Aunt Bess asked me to partner with Erica, so I did.

She was beautiful to me at the time, but looking back on it, she was way too skinny and pale. Doing lifts with her was like lifting a feather. We practiced three hours every day after school. And after dance practice was over, we practiced something else. I wasn't her first, so she taught me a lot."

"I see," said Jill starting to feel jealous. "Hey, poo happens. I'm not one to judge."

"Poo happens?" Nick was laughing.

"I thought the moment could use some levity, but go on with the story." She reached over and brushed a leaf from his hair.

"We won the dance competition, but after three or four months of practicing, he used air quotes with 'practicing', she found she was pregnant.

Right away she and her parents wanted an abortion. They had a dance career planned for her and they saw this as getting in the way. They were trying to climb the social ladder and were very snotty. What can I say? Aunt Bess went to my parents and persuaded them to fund Erica's education in whatever she chose to do. They also paid a tidy sum to Erica and her parents. She agreed to carry Anika for eight months *only*, at which time, she had a cesarean section and walked away forever."

"What a story!" exclaimed Jill. "So you raised Anika while you finished high school?"

"Not really," continued Nick. "Aunt Bess did the raising of Anika and of myself. I was only eight when I went to live with her, but that's another story. I learned to change diapers and feed her but aunt Bess did the rest. She never had any children so I think we made up for that in some way.

Once I was out of school, I went to college not too far away. On weekends I would go home and when I graduated...there was work. It was great until aunt Bess was murdered."

He heard Jill gasp and put both hands over her face. He related the rest of the events that took place that night and how he had made the decision to leave Anika in his parents care 'due to work obligations'. He still was not able to tell her of his real career as a concert pianist. He would have to, of course, but it just didn't seem like the right time yet.

"How about you, Jill. What's your story? Any skeletons in your closet? Boyfriends or husbands in the background?"

"No husbands," said Jill. "I was engaged once. To a 'New Yorker' no less. Geoffrey Beam, the third. As part of my training after I graduated culinary school, I spent a year in Italy working under a famous chef. Geoffrey would come in to the Italian bistro almost every day asking to speak to the chef and the chef would send me out. I think he saw himself as a matchmaker. He sucked at it, may I say. After a while, Geoff would show up with flowers or small gifts, etc., etc. You get the drift. Anyway, after a few weeks he asked me out, and I went." She paused and looked at the ground, her eyes hidden.

"You have to understand, Nick, I wasn't the prettiest girl in school and I've always had a little extra weight. Not a lot, but enough to be labeled 'fat' by the bullies in school. I was always taller than average and developed earlier than the other girls. That led to name calling of a different kind, if you know what I mean." Nick nodded his understanding.

"So I was very flattered by Geoff's attention. We dated for about six months and then he asked me to move in with him which was just a subtle way of asking me to have sex with him. I had some morals having been raised in a Christian home, so I told him I really wanted to wait until I was married. I was only twenty three at the time."

"Let me guess," said Nick. "He produced a ring."

"You got it," said Jill. "I bought it lock, stock, and barrel. The first night I was with him, he was so gentle with me. He held me afterwards while I cried. He told me it would get better each time. We lived together for only a couple of months when I realized he was tired of me or I couldn't please him. Either way, he started to stay out later and later and some nights he never came home. I told him I missed my family and was going back home to West Virginia. He didn't like that at all and it turned into one fight after another. He finally called me a fat, hillbilly 'has been' who was terrible in the sack and not worthy of his standing in society." She turned to watch a new group of rafters pass by.

"I was devastated. Too devastated to even return home. I decided to spend a year training in France, and then another year in Japan. I was so embarrassed at what I had done with Geoffrey that it took a long time and a lot of faith to finally return home. I had made a lot of money by saving and wining several cooking competitions over the years. I bought Mountain Mama's and the rest is history. I found some hard-won self- confidence and vowed never to let a fancy rich man turn my head ever again."

Nick didn't know what to say. He, for sure, wasn't going to tell her the rest of his story now. She was looking at him and waiting for his response.

"Jill, you are beautiful inside and out and I would like nothing more than to take you out and see where these feelings lead."

He drew her to him and planted soft kisses all over her face, her eyes, nose, cheeks and finally after what seemed like an eternity, her lips. After a few more, deeper kisses, Nick pulled back.

"Babe, I am confident that you are not terrible in the sack," He smiled teasing her with that statement but then he became serious again.

"I would never compromise your values or your faith. I wish I had the faith that you have. And having a family that is there for you and loves you no matter what…I can't even imagine what that is like. You've seen and heard what my family dynamic is like and it's pretty sad."

"I'm sorry, Nick," said Jill. "You deserve better. But it sounds like you're getting a second chance to have the family you've always wanted or get to know them better." She paused. "Or meet them for the first time." She laughed and dodged his playful punch to the arm.

"No, really, I think there is a piece of the puzzle missing from this story. I'll be praying that soon your dad will spill the beans."

"I'll be trying to pray too," said Nick.

"Nick, I am so glad to hear that!" She laid back against the rock and pulled Nick down to her. He was so close, they could have been one. Deep kisses followed, and a few moans here and there, but when she tried to pull him over on top of her, he pulled back, breathless. She was too.

"There's definitely chemistry here," he said.

"Definitely," agreed Jill. "So, maybe we should change the subject for a while. How about we go back to the festival and have a different kind of fun?"

"Yeah, maybe, but what about us?" he asked.

"I think we need to take this really slow, get to know each other and see what develops," she suggested. "If it's God's will in our lives, this thing between us will continue to grow and as it does, we keep asking for His guidance."

"Okay," said Nick. "I can live with that." He gave her one more quick kiss and helped her to her feet.

They found a ride back to the festival area with a guy driving a golf cart. They talked off and on about trivial things.

"Matt is really talented and I think he could make a living with his music," stated Nick.

"I'm sure of it," said Jill. "Ultimatly, he wants to teach at the college level and maybe be an orchestra conductor. He writes a fair amount of music. Really good stuff. He's young. He'll figure out God's plan for him. He's genius level, you know."

"I figured as much. My Anika is as well, but she only plays the violin. I tried to teach her piano but she never really took to it. Maybe I'm just a lousy teacher," he said.

"Well, if you only dabble in it, how could you hope to teach her, especially if she's genius level?" Jill shook her head at him.

Here was his opening to tell her who he really was, but again, he chickened out. "Hey, I'm genius level too, but just barely."

"Is that so?" Jill had a gleam in her eye like she didn't believe him.

"Yes. *Really*. My IQ is One hundred and forty on the nose."

"Well, you have me beat. Mine is only one thirty-five but Matt's is one seventy six," bragged Jill.

"Wow," said Nick "Anika's is one sixty-two. Any other genius's in your family?"

"Not as far as we know," said Jill.

"Mine neither," said Nick. "Actually, I really don't know that. Like you have found out, we really don't know each other."

They made it back to the top and spent the rest of the day looking around, eating greasy vendor food and holding hands. When they met up with the others, Brenda had joined them and Jill saw that she noticed the locked hands. Jill loved Brenda, but she could be really crude sometimes, especially for a school teacher.

"What have you two been up to all day?" asked Lorraine.

Brenda jumped in. "Doin' the nasty out in the woods!"

"Brenda! I beg your pardon," said Lorraine indignantly. "My daughter does not do 'the nasty' as you call it."

"Lorraine," said Nana. "When ye gotta go, ye gotta go. Ye can use leaves to wipe yer tukus but ye can get yer self a nasty rash and thorns in yer britches. That's why I just wear a diaper."

They all just stared at her. Brenda and Jill burst out laughing and Nick was bright red in the face. Jill knew it wasn't over. Brenda didn't miss much.

She leaned over and whispered to Jill. "Details, girlfriend, I want details!"

Jill gave her a look that said, 'mind your own business' and from that time on, they all talked about their day until the sun was setting and the time to leave was upon them.

Twelve

Nick was about halfway through the workday and having a hard time keeping his mind on what he was doing. He needed to finalize the plans for the indoor water park to give to his design team. He was hoping to draw in more tourists with this addition to the resort.

His mind kept drifting back to last weekend and how much he had enjoyed spending time with Jill. But his mind wasn't just on Jill. It was her whole family. He enjoyed being around them all. They were great. And his father! He still couldn't wrap his mind around that situation.

He also had a concert to perform in a little over two weeks in New York City. He was all set for that, at least. He always had a ready repertoire and had written a new piece for his daughter that he had never before performed. 'Anika's Theme'. As his mind went in that direction, suddenly he remembered that the parent-teacher conferences were this afternoon. He'd better get a move on if he was to remain on target.

Two hours later he was walking up the sidewalk and into his house. As he opened the door, he ran smack into Gerard. Nick had to grab the door frame to keep from falling backwards. Gerard, although shorter than Nick's six foot four, was solid as a rock.

"What the heck, Gerard! What are you doing here and how did you get in?"

"I still have the key you gave me at the groundbreaking ceremony and I tried to call but kept getting your voice mail."

Nick looked at his phone and saw he had three messages, all from Gerard. "What's going on?"

"I heard from Victor DeVille today on Alphonse Laurant's behalf. So we need to sit down with Jim and figure out our rebuttal or plan of action, if you will. I haven't been able to reach Jim either." Gerard looked aggravated as usual.

"Tonight is parent-teacher night at the high school and the Dennison's are probably there with Matt. Is Anika here? We were supposed to be there five minutes ago."

Gerard said, "I haven't seen her and I've been here for forty five minutes."

"Great!" said Nick. He started texting her and she answered back saying she was already there.

"Come on, let's go," said Gerard. "I can catch Jim there."

"And you can meet your niece's teachers," Nick said sarcastically.

"Oh, sure, that too," Gerard responded. He was already texting away and had lost interest in the conversation.

I've really got to get her a car, he said to himself.

Jill was in full Mountain Mama costume ready for the show to begin. She had a local guest chef from Beckley and

Aunt Shirley was filling in for Lorraine who was with Matt at the school. It had been one of those days when everything had been one step forward and two steps back. She had not slept very well since Bridge Day. That was also the last time she had talked with Nick.

She was having a war within herself. All the old feelings she'd had when she was with Geoffrey were flooding back into her thoughts and dreams. The guilt, the shame, and how hurt she had been. *Would Nick shake her off too when he realized just how 'West Virginia' she really was?* She was falling hard for Nick. She knew it, but she couldn't help it. He was gorgeous, kind to her family, a good father, and she could go on and on.

How could she have let herself fall for another man that she suspected was hiding something? She also suspected he was anything but poor. She didn't know what kind of income a project manager made, but from his car and home, he wasn't hurting for money. And she knew his family was wealthy.

She was worried about Nana as well. She was having an 'off' day and aunt Gladys and Josie were supposed to be watching her. However, she was just sitting at a table watching the birds out the window.

She had to get her head back in the game or she would have another disaster of a show like the one she'd had with Nick. Although they were still getting phone calls on that one. The public's interest had seemed to wane in the wake of that show.

As she heard the opening music start, she shook her head to clear it and thought that maybe it was time for a few changes in her life.

Nick and Gerard caught up with Anika at the school entrance.

"Don't tell me, let me guess," said Nick. "Matt gave you a ride."

"Actually, I never left school. I just hung around waiting for conferences to start and I tutored a freshman in math," she answered.

"Good girl," said Nick, "But next time, could you call and let me know?"

"Why?" said Gerard. "You don't check your messages." He saw the Dennison's at the end of the hallway. "Nick, I'm going to speak with Jim for a minute. We all need to meet *today*. I'll catch up with you in a few." He took off down the hall.

Nick followed Anika to her first class which was music history with Jill's friend, Brenda. Hard to believe she was a school teacher with her 'colorful' mouth and outspoken manner. But maybe in this day and age, that made for a better connection with the students.

Another student was already in the room, so they took a chair outside the door to wait their turn. Gerard caught up with them just as the other student was exiting the room.

"We're all going to meet at the restaurant for dinner as soon as this nonsense is over to go over the requests," said Gerard.

"Requests?" asked Nick.

They had not noticed that Brenda had come to the door and heard part of their conversation. *This can't be good, thought Nick.*

"What do you mean, *nonsense?*" She directed this to Gerard.

He responded with, "I don't have to explain myself to you. I don't have any children, hence, I'm not here for the conferences." He spoke to her slowly, as if he were speaking to a child.

"Hallelujah and thank the Lord for small favors! Kindly refrain from referring to this as nonsense since you obviously have not a single clue as to what goes on here or why," she stated emphatically. "Please come in, Nick and Anika, and I'm sorry, Anika, that you had to witness my abruptness."

"Wouldn't be the first time, Miss Montgomery," stated Anika.

"Anika! Your manners!" said Nick. "Brenda, this is my brother, Gerard Wallace, and Gerard, this is Jill's friend and Anika's music history teacher, Brenda Montgomery."

"I'd like to say it's nice to meet you, but I'll reserve judgment for now," said Brenda. "So, in or out, Gerard, what's it going to be?"

"I won't dignify that with a response," but he followed Nick in.

In a more professional tone of voice than Nick had ever heard, Brenda explained how her grading system worked, what they were studying, and how well Anika was doing. Anika was restless and asked to be excused from the room when she saw one of her friends in the hallway.

Nick started to thank Brenda for her time when she spoke.

"So, are you going to tell her?"

"Tell who, what?" Gerard butted in.

"Was I talking to you? Huh? *Was I talking to you,*" Brenda almost yelled. Gerard looked shocked. No one *ever* spoke to Gerard that way or questioned anything he said. Nick thought it was funny and Gerard had it coming. Gerard was always in control but Nick was used to Brenda's crude manner. *He's met his match thought Nick.*

Finally, Gerard said, "no, I don't believe you were talking to me."

"No, I was not, and I would thank you to keep your snoot out of other people's business!" said Brenda. Gerard just stood there looking at her.

Brenda turned her attention back to Nick and raised her eyebrows at him. Nick cleared his throat.

"So, you know," he stated.

"I finally recognized you. I have some of your CDs for Pete's sake," she said. "So are you telling her or am I?"

"Now who's butting in where they don't belong?" Gerard stated as arrogantly as he could.

Brenda was not as tall as Jill, but she drew herself up to her full height and slowly stepped towards Gerard. Nick stepped in between them.

"I plan on telling her and before you ask, I do know her story. I also know I could stand to lose any chance with her."

Brenda softened a little. "So you do want a chance with her. I'm glad, and Nick, if *anyone has a chance with her*, it's you. However, I would tell her sooner rather than later."

"I will," he said and turned to leave the room.

Brenda exited the room before Gerard and started yelling down the hallway.

"Here kitty, kitty. Here kitty!"

They both looked at her but she only had eyes for Gerard.

"I'm calling the cat to come and remove what he dragged in." She went back in the room and slammed the door.

"Are all the women here in West Virginia like that?" asked Gerard.

"Too soon to tell," answered Nick.

After the conferences, Nick and Gerard went to meet the others at Mountain Mama's. Nick had had to suffer a barrage of outrage about that 'fool woman' all the way there. Anika had ridden with Matt, thank you, Jesus!

Jill had just finished the show and was still in full costume. They all gathered at a table in the studio and Nick noticed that Nana was sitting over by a window just looking out. She seemed to be oblivious to everyone around her.

"Hi Nana," said Nick. "What are you doing over here all by yourself?"

Without looking up at him she said, "I'm a watchin' two old crows a sittin' on the back porch a talkin' to each other."

"Oh?" said Nick humoring her. "What are they talking about?"

"They're a sayin,' "This is as good as it gets." Then she got up and left leaning heavily on her cane.

He felt a little concerned. "Jill, is Nana okay? She has a blank look about her and she seems a little down."

"Nana has good and not so good days. She got the diagnosis of Alzheimer's about eight months ago and although it is a slow moving illness for most, we are seeing more and more short term memory loss. If she hadn't hidden away that letter from Victor DeVille in the first place, we wouldn't be dealing with this fallout now. But she can't help it. Having your dad here has been really good for her so I'm going to see this as one thing God is turning around for good."

Jill took his hand and led him to the table with the others, but Nick couldn't help feeling a little sad over this news.

Andrew and Jim had been conferring with Gerard about the 'Alphonse Incident' as they had been calling it, when Nick and Jill joined them. They all put in their dinner orders with Marlene before Jim began to speak.

"Okay," Jim began. "Alphonse has a list of demands that he is insisting on. Unless each one is met to his satisfaction, he says he will sue us all for every penny we've got."

"That's a bunch of hogwash," said Andrew. "But he can stir up a lot of trouble. He's known for it."

Jill, who was still in costume said, "let's start with his list of demands."

"I am having a really hard time having a serious discussion with you in that ridiculous outfit." Gerard directed his comment to Jill. "Can you, at least, remove the wig?"

"Fine," said Jill removing the wig. "What does he want?"

"First," said Gerard, "he wants a banquet held in his honor, you know, black tie, formal. Second, he wants a song written for him and played at the New York Symphony Orchestra concert in two weeks. Third, he wants an article written explaining what happened and a public apology in a major New York newspaper and a major magazine. He wants it to state that he is the only injured party here and this was a deliberate act against him. Forth, he wants Mountain Mama present at the banquet and concert and she must also watch a real chef, him, at work in his own kitchen."

Jill started to laugh while Nick looked shocked. After a few minutes she realized she was the only one laughing. She got herself under control. "Is he serious? This has got to be his idea of a joke."

"He is very serious," said her father.

"Okay, let's break it down," said Andrew. "The banquet is no problem. Ridiculous, but no problem. Honor him for what I can't imagine, but still, no problem. I can get Gwen on it right away. She can have a posh, formal affair together in two weeks with plenty of guests. Nick, I know you can take care of the second request so that won't be a problem either."

Nick was starting to sweat thinking his father would expose him right here in front of everyone.

"Interesting. You must know all the right people in all the high places to accomplish that," said Jill.

"Trust me," said Gerard. "If anyone can take care of that request, it's Nick."

"If you say so," said Jill.

Andrew continued, 'I think I can have a friend of mine write the article, but we'll save that for last. We're all going to pray that God will turn all this around for good."

Nick was surprised to hear his father say the same thing that Jill had prayed a couple of weeks ago. She had also made the same reference to Nana's situation a few minutes ago.

"And last, Jill, will you agree to go to New York and watch him cook? Maybe you can teach him a thing or two," asked Andrew.

They were all staring at her waiting for an answer. "Sure, why not?" She spoke offhandedly. "If it'll keep all of us out of hot water, I'll agree to the terms that involve Mountain Mama. It sounds like what he is really looking for is to simply humiliate Nick and I."

"I think that is his real intention," agreed Nick.

"So we have a plan," stated Gerard. "I'll call Victor tomorrow and tell him it's a go." He paused a minute and looked from Nick to Jill. "You are all smart. I'll bet you can come up with something to turn the tables on him, so my money's on you two."

That was as close to a compliment as Nick had ever heard from his brother and when he looked at Jill, she gave him big wink. He grinned and gave her one back.

They had all just finished eating when Matt came to the table and asked Nick if they could speak privately. Nick followed Matt out to the deck where he and Anika had been practicing their violins. Anika left to go ask Jill about helping her pick out a car and as soon as she was gone Matt turned to Nick.

"Sir, I know who you are."

Nick considered that. "Did Anika tell you?"

"No sir. I recognized you almost at once. I have some of your CDs and so does Jill but she hasn't listened to them in a while. Now that I think about it, I'm not sure they *are* hers. I think they may have belonged to that ex-fiance of hers. Anyway, I'm sure she doesn't know."

Matt looked away and Nick could see his face turning pink. "Sir, what I really wanted to speak with you about is some music I have been writing and to get your opinion, if you would oblige me."

"Of course," said Nick.

Matt picked up his violin and began to play the most beautiful piece Nick had heard in many years.

"You wrote that?" asked Nick.

"Yes sir. A couple of nights ago. Anika mentioned her birthday was coming up in a couple of months, so I thought I'd write something for her. I call it 'Anika's Theme'."

Nick was astounded! "You wrote that in only a couple of days?"

"Yes sir. What do you think?"

"I'm blown away and I have an idea. I've been writing an 'Anika's Theme' as well which I plan to play at the New York concert in a couple of weeks. I think what *you* have written and what *I* have written could be combined to be an unbelievable piano and violin duet. What do you say?"

"Really? Me… play in New York City with the most famous pianist of our time? *Heck, yeah!*"

They high fived a few times and Nick said, "I'd like for you to come over to my house tonight and we can play around with it. Also, just so you know, I plan to tell Jill before this thing between us goes any farther. How about I get Jill and we meet at my place in fifteen?"

"Sounds great! And can we not tell Anika? I think it would be a great surprise," said Matt.

Nick agreed and asked Jill to come over to his place with the kids and Gerard.

"I have something I would like to explain and I would like to do it on my own turf."

"Sounds ominous," said Jill. "Can I change first?"

"Sure. I need to talk to your dad for a few minutes anyway," and he wandered over to where the others were still talking.

Jill went upstairs to change and when she returned, Gerard had a look of relief on his face. "I can't get over that transformation!"

She ignored him and called to her dad. "I just got a call from Riley Tucker. She has the flu and can't play the piano tomorrow night. Mom can't do it because Nana isn't feeling well and Matt has another obligation."

Nick saw his chance. "What about me?" They all turned to look at him.

"Ahhh… that's not happening," said Jill. "I need someone who does more than 'dabble' on the piano. She noticed Gerard gave her a stern look and Matt looked very uncomfortable.

Just as well he thought. He didn't have a repertoire of 'mountain music' at the ready anyway.

She continued. "I'll call Brenda. She can play and sing."

"Lovely woman, by the way," spat Gerard. "Maybe I'll stick around to see another performance by 'her majesty'."

Jill just gave him a funny look and questioned Nick about that statement.

He just said, "I'll tell you later."

Matt asked Anika to grab his violin off the deck so he could take it with him to her house. He was about to tell Jill that he would be back early to help Brenda out when an ear splitting scream sounded from the deck. Anika came flying through the door and jumped right into Matt's arms. He caught her and would have fallen backwards himself if Gerard hadn't grabbed his shoulders to hold him up. She was clinging to Matt and crying. Josie ran in from the other room and Nick was by her in an instant.

"What happened," shouted Nick.

"It was awful!" Anika was sobbing. "It came running at me...it was going to attack! It stood on it's hind legs and bared it's fangs...it was just awful!" She clung to Matt and cried harder while he patted her back.

"Was it a bear?" asked Jim. "Josie, go get the bear gun."

Nick looked out the door with Jim right behind him carrying a huge shotgun.

"I don't see anything."

The others followed behind him. Josie shined a spot light around and after a few minutes they started to laugh. Gerard finally wandered out.

"Anika," said Jill, "is this what tried to attack you?"

Matt tried to put her down but she clung harder. Gerard looked at where the spot light was shining.

"What is that? I don't see any fangs."

Andrew came out and slapped Gerard on the back. They were still laughing when Andrew repeated, "Anika, honey, is this what tried to attack you?"

"No! I can't look! It was six feet tall with bloody fangs and claws ready to take my face off!" She continued to cry. "I tell you, it was ten feet tall and lunged at me!"

Nick tried to stop laughing. "Anika, it is just a possum."

"No dad! It was twelve feet tall and dragging a dead body!"

"Matt, put my niece down! Not everyone has seen a possum!" Gerard stalked away as Gerard tended to do.

~

A short time later, they were all at Nick's house and Jill announced that everything was all set for Brenda to entertain the next evening.

"Wow!" said Jill. "This place rocks! It's beautiful! And so well laid out! You could do so much with this place."

"Are you saying I haven't?" asked Nick with a smile.

Jill poked him in the ribs at the same time she saw the grand piano in the back by the huge bay windows.

"I thought you said Anika doesn't play?"

"She doesn't," replied Nick. "I told you that I play."

"You dabble," said Jill. "That is what you said."

"Let's all go and look at cars on the internet so my sister and Nick can talk in private," said Matt loudly. "You too, Gerard, we need your help."

They all followed Anika into the office area and left Jill and Nick alone.

"Another skeleton coming out," said Jill.

"I'm afraid so, the last of it's kind," said Nick a little sadly. "I don't know how to put this without upsetting you.I should have told you before this, but it never seemed like the right time and for that, I apologize."

"Just let me have it," said Jill getting irritated.

"Have you noticed our names are all shortened from a longer name? Sort of like a nick name, pardon the pun."

"No. I can't say I've put any thought into it."

"Take Gerard, that is short for…bad example. He's just Gerard. No one has had the nerve to give him a nick name, although we could all think of some," said Nick nervously.

"I sense stalling going on," said Jill. "Out with it."

"How about Gwen. What would you say Gwen is short for?"

"Gwendolyn, I suppose," said Jill.

"No, it's short for Guinevere."

"Different," said Jill. "So far, so good."

"How about Rod?" His face was starting to turn red and his palms were sweating.

"Rodney," said Jill starting to grow bored with this game.

"Nope. Roderick," replied Nick.

"How about Nick?"

"I'm guessing it's not Nicolas," said Jill.

"It's Nicolai," said Nick waiting for the fallout.

She stared wide eyed at him, then at the piano. Then back at him putting two and two together.

"Shut up!" She almost screeched. "No way! Nicolai…the famous Nicolai…*the world famous Nicolai?!* That explains why writing a song and playing it for Alphonse is not a problem for you! Oh my God! How did I not see it! I don't believe it!" She was slowly backing away.

Nick sat down at the piano and started playing a complicated piece. He was hoping she would be entranced like most who heard him play. He glanced at her and she was staring open mouthed at him just shaking her head. *Were those tears on her cheeks?*

He closed his eyes and played from his heart another song he had written. 'My Heart for Jill'. He was not planning on revealing it yet. He continued to play until he heard the loud slamming of the front door. He stopped and sat quietly at the piano feeling like his heart was gone as well.

Thirteen

Nick sat at the piano with his hands still on the keys but he had stopped playing.

"Lord," he prayed out loud. "I know you haven't heard much from me over the last few years, but I would like to change that. I need your guidance and strength to get through whatever is coming my way. I need wisdom and insight on the events that are to take place in New York and in my relationship with Jill. Please give me the right words to say to make this right. In Jesus name…"

"Amen," said Matt who had refrained from interrupting the prayer.

"I thought I was alone," said Nick. "I'm not used to praying, not for a long time now."

"That was straight from the heart. I could hear your sincerity and I know the Lord does too," said Matt coming over to the piano. "What happened with Jill?"

"She stormed out the front door. Slammed it hard. I felt it all the way over here."

"She'll be back. Give it…ohhh…say thirty minutes or so. She probably left because she was embarrassed more than anything else. She had just *turned you down* to play at the restaurant. She's feeling *blindsided*. Maybe a little hurt and thinking you didn't trust her enough to tell her. She's more than likely mad at herself for not recognizing you." Matt paused thoughtfully.

"She'll call Brenda and hash it out and pace for a while. Maybe even call Aunt Shirley and blow off steam. Not much fazes her but this was too much. I think the worst part for her is that she's going to think she was the only one who didn't know."

"Matt, you sure sound like you know your sister and I hope you're right and she does come back. It's just as well she turned me down. I don't know any country or blue grass music that I could have played off the top of my head. Of course, I could have played by the sheet music, no problem. But you need to feel it to inspire others to feel it. That's the difference in playing the notes and playing the music."

"I understand completely, sir, and so does your daughter," said Matt. "But I bet you know more than you think. You just don't realize it. We also play gospel and some more popular music. How about 'Sweet Home Alabama', 'Old Man River', or 'Amazing Grace'?"

"You are a very wise and intuitive young man, Matt." Nick began to play a lengthy intro into 'Amazing Grace'.

He glanced up to see Anika and Gerard had joined them and he began to sing the words in a rich baritone. Matt joined in singing harmony and playing a counter melody on the violin. Anika joined in with her pleasant alto as Gerard rolled his eyes and left the room mumbling something about 'possums'.

They played and sang for a while and finally took a break to have a snack in the kitchen. Gerard was at the table with his laptop and noticed Nick checking his messages.

"I guess you have to be a beautiful, curvy, non-related redhead to get your messages noticed," said Gerard in a snotty tone.

"So, you think Jill is beautiful?" Nick asked his brother.

"Duh," said Gerard. "But you should have told her right from the start about your status."

"He's right, dad. I hope you didn't just ruin my relationship with her too. She was going to go car shopping with me," whined Anika.

"This has nothing to do with you, honey," said Nick. "I'm sure nothing will change towards you."

"Good, because next weekend I get to play my violin on family night," she continued.

"That's going to be different from the norm. When was this decided upon," asked Nick.

"Well, it just sort of happened. I practice with them a lot so they asked me to play on family night and I said 'yes'."

"Sir," said Matt. "She's great and she fits right in. You'll love it. I hope you say it's okay."

"Of course it is," said Nick. "I'll be there this time to see you all in action. At least, I hope I will, if Jill ever speaks to me again."

"Oh, she'll speak to you again, as a matter of fact, right now!" No one had heard Jill enter.

"I think it's time for me to leave," said Matt. He shook Nick's hand and nodded to Anika. He hugged Jill and spoke in her ear.

"Go easy on him, sis. He's a great guy and I think you'll regret it for the rest of your life if you don't work this out."

Anika gave her dad a hug and said she had a test to study for. She turned to Jill.

"Are we still on for our car shopping date Monday after school?"

"Of course," she replied. She ran to Jill and gave her a hug. She whispered so only Jill could hear.

"Please make up with him. You are the best thing for him. For us!" With that, she turned and ran up the stairs.

"I'm so sorry for not telling you sooner," Nick began.

"You really should have," said Gerard helping himself to the fruit bowl. "I told you so."

"Can we have some privacy, please?" Nick was feeling aggravated toward Gerard.

"Oh, sure, but if she kicks you to the curb, you can only blame yourself!"

"Thanks so much for the input, Gerard," Nick said on a sarcastic note.

"Not a problem. Anytime." And he went up the stairs to his room.

When they were alone she said, "I did some thinking and some praying after I walked out. I talked to Brenda and Aunt Shirley a little bit too."

Man, that Matt is right on the money so far, Nick thought to himself.

Jill continued. "It's not that you are who you are, it's just that I feel like a fool for not realizing it. Am I the only one that didn't know?"

"I didn't tell anyone. As far as I know, Brenda and Matt are the only ones that figured it out and I didn't find that out until a couple of days ago."

Nick continued his explanation.

"When I first got into town, I didn't even know if anyone here would have heard of me, let alone, recognize me. It's not like I'm in every magazine or television show. Yes, a lot of people know who I am, but I have done very few performances over the last few years and haven't recorded any new music for even longer than that. And I don't announce myself when I arrive in a new location. That's Alphonse Laurant's game, not mine."

"I feel really let down, for lack of a better description. But I guess after you heard about my situation with Geoffrey and my announcement about how I would never become involved with that kind of man again, you must have felt you couldn't say much. At least according to Brenda. She thinks I should let you off the hook."

"Smart gal, that Brenda," said Nick with some of his hope returning.

"I'm not sure where we go from here," said Jill. "I think we should back things off for now and just let all of this drama settle."

"If that's how you feel, I won't impose my company on you," Nick said a little stiffly.

"I just need some time to digest all this," said Jill. "I still plan to take Anika to pick out her car, but don't you need to be there to sign for it?"

"Not really," said Nick. "Let her pick out what she wants as long as it isn't too flashy and it's suitable for a teenage girl. I am aware that Anika likes to stand out a bit. Here's my credit card. Anika can sign on it."

Jill was just starting to realize how rich this dude really was. Filthy rich, she would almost bet on it. She wasn't too sure she was ready to go down that road again. Yet, she didn't want him to change who he was, just for her, just like she wouldn't want to change who she was just for him.

I think there's a lesson to be learned here, Lord. Help us both to understand your will. Jill took the card and put it in her purse.

"Would you mind doing me another favor? You've been out to the job site and know the road conditions in the winter better than I do. Would you be willing to pick out a truck for me also? Something suitable for the area and not too flashy. I've never owned a truck before. The Jag is just not going to make it up the hill without major damage before too much longer."

Nick almost begged her to help him out. He also knew it was probably too much to ask given their circumstances.

Jill thought for a moment and finally leaned on the piano with her arms crossed. "You do need a truck or at least a four wheel drive. Will you be hauling supplies?"

"No, probably not. I just need to get up and down the mountain roads and into the job site without getting stuck," he replied.

"Okay, I can do that for you if you trust me," she said. "I'll get dad's input as well. What price range are we talking?"

"Price is no object," he stated realizing too late how that must sound to her.

"Of course it isn't," Jill said testily.

"I really didn't mean for it to come out sounding that way."

Jill lowered her head and took a deep breath before she spoke.

"I know you didn't and I'm sorry for being such a brat, but you deserve it for not being honest with me from the start."

Nick looked at her with a smile.

"How about this for a first meeting……Hello there, beautiful, I'm Nicolai Wallace, world famous pianist. I'm a great catch, stinking rich, with so much money, I'll never be able to spend it all, and you should bow at my feet because everyone else does! Would that have been better?"

"Okay, okay!" Jill was laughing. "I guess it sucks to be you! No, seriously, though, it must be hard to find someone who wants you for yourself and not for your money."

"That is very true. Another reason I wanted out of New York City. I wanted Anika to spend the last couple of years in school with normal kids. Being around my mother for the last four years, caused some misconceptions about wealth and using others for your own benefit."

Jill changed the subject. "You know, Anika is going to play her violin next weekend for family night."

"Yes, she told me and I'm okay with it," he said. "I can't picture how that will fit in, but you know your venue better than I."

Nick quickly changed the subject when Jill clearly wanted to discuss it further. "Let me tell you a secret."

He filled her in on the music he and Matt would be playing together at the concert in New York. They were still working the kinks out but Nick felt it might have the potential to be recorded at some point.

"That's wonderful! I know Matt must be beside himself! That is such a great thing to do for him," she exclaimed.

"He deserves it. He's a great kid and I don't mind saying, he reminds me a little of myself at that age… except for the daughter thing," he tacked on at the last minute. "Maybe while we are there, I'll show him around Julliard."

"Don't tell me, let me guess. You went there too," said Jill a little sarcastically.

"It's my Alma Mater, I'm proud to say, and I hope it will be Anika's too." He could tell she was getting a little irritated with the conversation so he started to softly play an old hymn.

She looked like she was starting to relax again so he took another step, pushing down his shyness, he began to sing the words. She looked very surprised but she smiled in that beautiful way he just loved. She could light up the room with that smile. When he got to the chorus she joined him singing harmony.

"Then sings my soul, my Savior God to Thee."

They continued to play and sing old hymns until they heard Gerard yell down the stairs.

"Will you two knock it off for the night! Some of us are trying to sleep!"

Nick smiled and stopped playing. "I guess that's it for tonight," he said while he carefully closed the lid over the piano keys.

"We make a great duet for singing," said Jill.

"That's not all we're great at together," said Nick. "But I'll leave that subject alone for now." He gave her a wink while she reached out and touched his cheek. Then she turned around and left.

~

At work on Monday, Nick sat at one of the tables that were set up for the site workers to eat their meals. He was doing some reflecting on the events of the last few days. He didn't think Jill was going out of her way to avoid him, but she was always busy when he was around.

He and Gerard had gone to Mountain Mama's on Friday evening to eat dinner and catch part of Brenda's performance. Even though it was Gerard's idea in the first place, all he did was grumble about 'the horrid woman'.

It was entertaining enough but Gerard made a comment a little too loud.

"She's no Nicolai".

Unfortunately for him, he had said it loud enough for Brenda to hear, and in that wake came a group of songs she seemed to be directing at him. Matt had joined her on the last few songs taking over on the piano while she sang 'Hit The Road, Jack' and 'These Boots Were Made For Walking'.

The diners had found it very entertaining. Especially at the end when she plopped down on Gerard's lap, grabbed his face and planted a big kiss on his shocked lips. Then she had bowed and sashayed out of the room swinging her hips in an exaggerated fashion.

After that, Nick had driven a silent Gerard to the airport to catch the next flight to Chicago. Nick had to smile every time he thought about that.

Nick and Anika had attended church the following Sunday, but Jill had sat with her family, and other than a quick wave, she had said nothing to him.

Mark and Nancy had been in town for family practice and Anika had been part of that. He, however, had not been invited. So he had spent the rest of the weekend at the resort site or at the piano perfecting his music for the coming concert. Matt was planning to meet him at his house later this evening and after school the rest of the week to work on Anika's Theme. Nick also was hoping that Matt would assist him in composing a song for Alphonse.

Nick was toying in his mind with some variation of 'Twinkle Twinkle Little Star' when he heard car horns blaring.

He looked behind him to see two unfamiliar vehicles heading down the hill towards the site. He had forgotten that today was the day Jill had taken Anika to pick up the car that she had purchased over the internet and refused to show him.

Note to self: do not give your credit card to your teenage daughter and say 'get whatever you want'.

He started walking to the parking area where the vehicles had come to a stop. Anika jumped out of a pale metallic lime green Volkswagen and came running to him.

"What do you think, dad? Isn't it awesome?"

Nick walked around the car and noticed she'd had a violin and musical notes airbrushed on both front doors. As he wondered how much that rush job had set him back, he realized this car was totally Anika. Not too flashy that it said 'I'm rich' but different enough that it let her stand out a little. He was pleased. He gave Jill a nod.

"Thank you".

He turned his attention to the vehicle Jill had driven over. It was a huge Hummer, navy blue with lots of shiny chrome. He walked over to it but wasn't sure he wanted to be seen in the thing.

He looked at Jill.

"It had 'Nick' written all over it!"

"No! You didn't!" He started walking around it looking for his name. Jill put a hand on his arm to stop him.

"Seriously, you're genius level? If I were you I'd call Julliard and ask for a refund."

She started to laugh at the look on his face. "You said you trusted me. It's solid, sturdy, four wheel drive, and very roomy inside. The navy blue matches your eyes and it's sexy, just like you."

"Oh! Gross!" Anika put her hands over her ears. "That's it. I'm out of here. I don't even want to hear the response to that!"

She climbed in her car and took off with the radio blaring just for good measure.

"Sexy huh? If that thing is sexy like me, I'd better throw the towel in now. There's no hope." But he was grinning.

"Come on. Let's take it for a spin. See how it handles on the mountain roads."

She handed him the keys and he climbed in the driver's seat. She was right. It was roomy and comfortable with so many gadgets and controls, he felt like he was in the cockpit of a plane.

They spent the rest of the afternoon driving the mountain roads as well as the country dirt roads. Finally, he dropped Jill off at Mountain Mama's. She had done a great job for both he and Anika. He owed her big time.

"I'd like to thank you for all of your work with this."

"It was no problem. We scoped things out on the internet first. Your dad found this and thought it would suit you."

All Nick could think of to say about that revelation was, "interesting".

"Jill, I was thinking, how about going to New York early on Thursday and do some shopping and sight-seeing? That will give us plenty of time before the banquet and concert on Saturday for me to treat you and Matt to a shopping spree for formal attire, as a way of thanking you for all your help. I have to get some newer things for myself and Anika anyway. We can even tour Julliard or wherever you'd like to go. Come on, it'll be fun. You all can stay in my suite at the Grand Wallace. There's plenty of room," he said hopefully.

She looked thoughtful for a minute then spoke.

"It sounds perfect except for the part about buying my clothing. I may not be 'Nick rich', but I do alright for myself. I will allow you to treat Matt, though. This is really special for him. *Thank you* for all you've done and this opportunity you've given him."

"No problem," said Nick.

Jill gave him another wave and he watched her until she was safely inside. Only then did he allow himself to acknowledge that he was falling in love with her.

Fourteen

The following Saturday night was family night at Mountain Mama's restaurant. The entertainment was by the Dennison family, primarily, and the seats had to be reserved in advance to be allowed in. The proceeds collected were always donated to various charities and tonight's proceeds would be going to the Alzheimer's Foundation in honor of Nana. Jill refused to let Nick purchase a ticket so he went to Lorraine and made a sizeable donation to the cause.

The stage area was set up in the main dining room of the restaurant and Nick noticed there were more instruments than usual present. He noticed there was a drum set...*hmmm... haven't seen that before.* There was an acoustic guitar as well as an electric one, the banjo, viola and electric bass. *Let's see...what else... jugs, spoons and a washboard.* He had not seen the whole group play together. He found he was excited but he couldn't see how Anika and her classical music would fit into this scenario. Impressive, but very far from their own venue.

He was looking over the limited menu used for these special occasions and trying to decide between the chicken fried steak and the country seafood platter when Rod walked in. Nick stood up and they shook hands.

"I didn't know you were coming," said Nick.

"Are you kidding? I wouldn't miss my nieces debut into country music for the world," said Rod. "Now that we have started to get to know each other, I just want to be around you guys all the time." Then he grinned and amended that statement.

"With the possible exception of Gerard."

"I know how you feel and I feel the same way. Anika is just going to play her violin. I haven't heard anything about her playing country music. Honestly, I don't think she knows any. I think she would have told me if she was playing their music, wouldn't she?" Nick looked to Rod.

"Hey man, how should I know, she's your daughter," Rod replied. "I guess we'll see soon."

They gave their orders and watched as the others started coming to the stage, setting up, and tuning their instruments. Lorraine was at the piano facilitating that. They were dressed in hillbilly type clothing with old jeans and hats as well as being unshaven and unkempt in general.

"Oh no! Anika's really going to stand out when she comes on," said Nick.

"Look, there's Josie!" He stood up and waved, getting a kiss blown to him in return.

"What's that about," asked Nick.

"Nothing. She's just a flirt, but she looks good in those tight jeans and that tiny shirt," said Rod. "We do texting and e-mail sometimes."

Nick saw the longing in his brother's eyes before he looked away. He saw Jill coming their way and she was wearing bib overall short shorts with an old tee shirt underneath. Her hair was curly and came down past her shoulders. She stopped at their table.

"Before you ask, hair extensions."

They all noticed Nana walking through the room stopping to talk to customers here and there. She was dressed in an old house dress and apron with what looked like combat boots.

"I hope Nana is up to this. She hasn't joined in for a while now," said Jill looking worried.

Nana was at the table next to Nick's when they saw her point her finger at the couple seated there.

"Pull my finger!"

Jill rushed over to grab her and apologize to the couple who knew Nana and understood her condition. Jill ushered her to the stool set up close to Lorraine at the piano and handed her the washboard.

Jill saw Nancy arrive and took her to sit with Nick and Rod.

"Can you two keep an eye on Nancy while we play? She's feeling a little puny tonight." Jill also noticed how pale she looked.

"I'm fine, really, but I'd just like to have a fruit plate if that's possible," she said.

"Sure," said Jill and she spoke into her phone. "Well, we're about ready to go on. Thanks again for letting Anika do this and like I tried to explain the other night, a little surprised to be honest."

Nick was about to respond.

"BAM!" A man had come up behind them and slapped his hand down on the table and yelled 'BAM' again. They had all jumped a foot, especially Nancy.

"Bam McGee, if I've told you once, I've told you a hundred times to stop sneaking up on people or I'll 'BAM' you out of here," stated Jill sternly.

"I'm sorry, Miss Jill, but I'm so excited I just can't help myself!" He started to move across the room when Jim stopped him and shook his hand.

"What's the good word, Bam?

Bam thought for a minute.

"You know them TV preachers I watch during the day?"

Jim nodded his head.

"Well, my dog don't like none of 'em."

"Is that right? Is that because he disagrees with their doctrine?" Jim tried not to laugh. Bam clearly didn't understand the question so he moved on across the room.

"He's harmless," said Jill laughing. "Just loud and you never know what he'll say next. He's a little off but no one really knows why. We all think he's sweet on Aunt Shirley, though. Don't tell her I said that!"

"BAM!" They all heard him across the room.

"I'd better run." She took her place on a stool behind the guitars.

Nick was having a hard time keeping his eyes off her legs. He saw Matt join the group, but still no sign of Anika.

Jim took the microphone and said a brief welcome to everyone in attendance.

Jim continued. "I'd like to introduce you to a new member of our family band. Please give a nice welcome to Andy Wallace!"

Nick looked over at Rod and saw that Rod was as surprised as he was. Andrew bounded onto the stage area. He took a seat next to Nana in the front and picked up what looked like spoons.

They heard 'BAM' across the room and Andrew responded with a wave and a 'BAM' of his own. Then they heard the opening of the first song with the men singing 'constant sorrow', then the instruments and other voices followed. It was very good with Andrew playing the spoons with expertise.

"And the surprises just keep on coming," said Rod.

"Yeah," said Nick. "What's next? Mother on the nose harp?"

"Or Gerard on the bag pipes?" Rod laughed. They high fived each other just as the song ended.

Jim took the mic again and began another short speech.

"We have another surprise for you tonight and this one is really special."

"Hey!" Andrew interrupted in an obviously rehearsed tone. "Are you saying I'm not special?"

"Bam".

"No, I'm kidding," said Andrew. This one is really special! Welcome my granddaughter little Annie Wallace!"

Anika jogged onto the stage wearing short shorts and a shirt tied around her waist. Her hair was in pig tails and she looked like she needed a good bath.

Nick started to stand and protest when he caught Jill's eye. She was looking at him like she didn't know why he looked shocked. Then he understood...he had been played again, by little 'Annie'. She had known he would protest, so she had given him just enough information with which to get by.

"Easy, man," said Rod. "Let's see what she can do. This doesn't mean she'll turn all hillbilly on you."

"I think she already has," but Nick sat back down.

Anika took her place next to Matt and Nick saw Matt wink at her.

She caught Nick's eye and looked away quickly. The song began with Matt playing the fiddle intro, then Mark joining in on the drums. Jim started singing the lead to 'The Devil Went Down to Georgia'.

Nick knew something was wrong right away. Anika was supposed to be playing and she wasn't. He knew it wasn't stage fright, it was him. She was feeling his disapproval.

Matt quickly jumped in to play and he knew he had to fix this. This was an intricate and difficult piece he told himself. Just because it wasn't Mozart didn't mean it had no musical merit.

Jill had the electric guitar solo and Nick had never seen anything so sexy. Josie followed on the electric bass and he saw Rod give her a big thumbs up. Matt was spot on with the Devil's fiddle part but he had a worried look on his face.

Just before Matt's part ended, Nick caught Anika's eye and gave her two thumbs up. He saw her relax and nod to Matt.

Johnny's portion of fiddle playing began and Anika was unbelievable. The last portion of the song Matt and Anika both played in perfect synch. Not a missed note from either one. Nick couldn't help it. He had tears in his eyes and had to wipe them away. Nancy took his hand and gave it a squeeze.

Nick was so proud of Anika and he felt like such a louse for making her feel like playing this kind of music was a big 'come down' from the classical music she had grown up playing. Nick realized he was a music snob.

They received a standing ovation when the song ended and Jim gave a yell.

"Let's hear it for little Annie Wallace!"

Nick stepped out of his comfort zone and stood up and whistled right along with Rod. Anika had the biggest smile on her face and Jill gave Nick a thumbs up as well.

"They are so good," said Rod.

"I had no idea," said Nick. "They should be recording."

Just then Jim announced that all of their CDs were available for purchase in the restaurant gift shop with all proceeds going to Alzheimer's research.

"Okay then," said Nick.

Jim announced the next song as a popular one from the seventies and would feature Nana.

Nick figured it would be a song from her youth but when they started to play, he saw Josie put a harmonica on a stand in front of her and heard the first strains of 'Black Water' with Nana singing the lead in a clear contralto.

Jill and Andy played the acoustic guitar parts and Matt and Anika had a nice fiddle duet. When the harmonica part came around, Josie played both the harmonica and the bass at the same time. Nick could see Rod was drooling over Josie and when the song ended, he and Rod stood and clapped and shouted as loud as anyone in the room. They heard another 'BAM' across the room and responded with a 'BAM' of their own. He could see Jill laughing from the stage.

The band played for another hour with the twins coming out to do some clogging and singing as well. At the end of the evening, they played an encore of 'The Devil Went Down to Georgia' and again, it was flawless. Everything ended with hooting and hollering and another standing ovation.

Mark came over to get Nancy and she gave him a big hug and kiss that went on for so long Rod felt the need to interject.

"Hey, get a room."

Mark pulled away. "Thanks guys for keeping an eye on my wife." He left to take Nancy upstairs to rest.

The others came over and Anika looked at Nick and then at Jill.

"I'm sorry for letting you think my dad was onboard with this. And dad, I'm sorry for not telling you but I thought you would tell me it was beneath my talent."

That hit him in the gut, but he had already realized that she was right. He felt very ashamed of himself.

"I can see both sides," said Jill. "But, Anika, if you want to keep playing with us you will have to be up front with your dad and myself from now on. No tricks, no omissions. Is that clear?"

"Yes ma'am. Very clear."

"And no rubbing your father's nose in it."

"Yes, ma'am,' she responded again.

Matt came over and they went to join the twins to get something to eat but not before she wrapped her arms around her father's neck.

"I love you."

Rod had gone to the stage to talk to Josie leaving Nick and Jill alone at the table.

"What did you think?" Jill was staring him down.

"Total shock at first with father playing the spoons. And when did he learn to clog? I also learned something about myself. I was holding my kind of music high above your kind of music and I'm sorry. That will never happen again. Your talent is just as great as any classical musician I've worked with. I feel very humbled right now."

Jill reached up and wiped at some moisture at the corner of Nick's eye, then licked it off her finger with her tongue.

"That was so hot," said Nick.

"I felt I needed to rescue you before you blubbered all over me, dude but yeah, I'm glad you thought it was hot," said Jill with a smile.

Andrew came over to them dragging Rod.

"Father, I'm in awe!" Nick shook Andrews hand. "What a performance!"

"Knock off the 'father' crap, both you boys. Call me dad or daddy or pa, anything but father. Makes me sound like a stiff old geezer. Personally, I prefer 'pappy' but I'll leave it up to you." He slapped them both on the back and bounded back across the room.

"Pappy?" All three said at the same time.

And Nick thought for the umpteenth time, *who is this man?*

Fifteen

Jill was going over last minute directions with her staff before leaving for New York in the morning. Technically, her mother was next in command but she would rather have her Aunt Gladys take the lead while she was gone. She explained it away to Lorraine by using Nana as an excuse. So far, Nana had refused any medication for her condition and Jill managed to talk Lorraine into scheduling an appointment for Nana with her doctor for this Friday to try to get her to reconsider.

Jill was not going to do a Mountain Mama show this week. She had decided to have Aunt Shirley and Jean do a cooking demonstration instead. Since Thanksgiving was only a few weeks away, she would use this opportunity to do a pilot for an idea she had been kicking around for a few weeks. Shirley and Jean would cook some favorite holiday dishes while engaging in mother and daughter bantering. They were experts at that and Jill thought it would be entertaining for the audience as well.

Matt and Nick had worked all week on Anika's Theme and the song for Alphonse. Both were done and although Jill had not heard either one, by Matt's excitement, she was sure they were brilliant.

She, however, was nowhere near ready. She hadn't packed a thing, but then, she did plan on buying a new wardrobe while she was in New York. This was her justification for not being on top of things.

She was usually so organized down to the last detail. *What was wrong with her?* Her mind kept going in so many different directions! She would be in New York for three days with Nick and the kids. She kept thinking about how Nick would view her when on his usual turf. All the beautiful women he would see, maybe even dated. She could never compete with them. Maybe she should back out. No, she was no coward! She was as good as any of those women. She had to keep telling herself that.

Then there was Matt. He had never been to a really big city before and she was so excited for the opportunity that Nick was giving him. What if Nick decided not to let Matt play when he saw him against the crème of society in the orchestra. Matt was only eighteen for Pete's sake! He would be crushed! What would she say to Nick?

Stop it Jill! Stop it, stop it, stop it! She had to cut this business out. This was not her style. What had gotten into her? *Dear Lord, Help*!

She had gotten very little sleep lately because all she could think of was Nick and what he might really think of her. They had chemistry but was that all there was? Would the skinny blondes win in the end? Okay, on to things that had to be done or needed to be thought about.

They were flying, but she had no idea what time they had to be at the airport. Hopefully Nick bought the tickets because she had no time to do that. She would pay him back later. Hair and make-up! She had better take stock to see if she was out of anything, but then again, it was too late to run to the store to get any.

Lord help her, she would probably have to meet Nick's mother. No point in wasting time thinking about that. She already knew she would not measure up with her and neither would Matt. Her own children didn't even make the cut. She hadn't considered the weather! What was New York like this time of year?

She sat down at a table in the studio and put her head in her hands. She couldn't concentrate and she really needed to. She looked up and saw Nana headed her way. She took a seat across from Jill.

Nana looked into Jill's eyes.

"Somethin's stuck in yer craw and I bet I know what's a eatin' at ye, girl."

"And what's that, Nana?" Jill tried to rein in her impatience.

"Ye can't get yer mind off'n yer feller. What a fine piece of horse flesh he is."

Jill put her head down on the table. "Oh, Nana, I don't know what to do!"

"Great day in the mornin' child! Ye do what comes naturally. Them things aren't hard to figger out! I thought at yer age you'd know what to do an where babies come from. Why, when I was yer age I knew all kinds of tricks to make the fellers come back fer more, I did"

"No, Nana! I need to know what to do about my heart. I've gone and fallen in love with Nick!"

Nana threw her head back in glee and slapped the table. "I knowed it, I knowed it plain as day. And he's in love with you too. I can see it written all over his face, I can."

"Do you really think so, Nana?"

"I've knowed it fer a spell now. Ye each light up when ye see the other," she said. "Jill, all ye have to do is jest be yerself. Nobody else. It's who he fell fer. Not some high falutin' debutante. Ye jest need to be Jill."

"Thank you, Nana. I love you." Jill kissed her weathered cheek.

"Gw'on now an make me some purty great grandchildren. It's not hard but it will be when ye get the hang of it, you mark my words." Nana laughed at her own joke.

Jill looked confused, then it hit her. "Nana! I don't believe you just said that!"

Nana let out another big guffaw.

"Do it, girl, do it!" And she went over to sit in her favorite spot by the window.

Jill's mind felt a little clearer and she quickly made a list of things she still needed to do.

As she was heading upstairs to start packing, Anika came in the front door.

"You aren't working today, are you sweetie?" asked Jill.

"No, I'm here to give Matt a couple of dance lessons. He says he can't dance and there *will* be dancing at the banquet," said Anika.

Jill thought for a moment and knew very well that Matt was a great dancer. Had his feelings for Anika changed?

"Anika, I can't dance very well, either. Geoffrey and I went dancing a few times but Nick is on a whole different level."

"Come on with me," she said. "I'll teach you both a couple of simple dances and don't worry, dad's great at leading."

"Did I hear my name?" Nick entered from the restaurant area.

"Yes dad, you did," she said to Nick. "I'm going to teach Matt some simple dances and it seems that Jill needs a lesson as well."

"I'm up for it'" said Nick following Anika up the stairs.

They followed her into the larger banquet room where Matt had music already playing.

"I wondered if you'd show up, sis. I don't think you can dance any better than me," said Matt kidding around with her.

"Thanks a lot, Matt," said Jill and then she saw him wink at her. What was up, she wondered.

"Okay, okay," said Nick. "We'll try a simple waltz and if that goes well, we'll move on to the Viennese Waltz and maybe a foxtrot. Come on, *'Annie'*, let's show them."

Nick and Anika demonstrated an almost perfect Viennese Waltz and a few other dances as well. Matt was watching very intently. He wasn't taking his eyes off Anika. Jill knew the feeling. She couldn't keep her eyes off Nick either. The way he moved...so sensual! Oh, she was in trouble!

"Okay," said Nick. "It's time for you two to give it a shot."

Nick worked with Jill and Anika worked with Matt. He'd almost bet Matt had done some dancing of some sort or at least practiced up a bit. Jill wasn't bad herself. A natural. Or maybe they just fit so well together that they had a natural flow about them. Or maybe just chemistry. They practiced for the next two hours until Jill had done a remarkable Viennese Waltz as well as a couple more complicated dances.

"That's it for me," said Matt shaking the sweat from his hair. "I still have to pack and I'm starved. Come on Annie, let's go eat." And the two of them left still full of energy.

"I still have a few things to do also," said Jill. "What time are we leaving in the morning?"

"I've asked Josie to drive us to the airport a little before nine. Once we're in the air it will only take about forty-five minutes to get to the city. I'm excited! I'm really looking forward to being there with you."

Nick was looking at her very intently, his dark blue eyes locked on her light gray ones. Jill was drawn to him but was trying very hard to fight the attraction. The way he moved. He was so graceful and so sexy. He made her feel sexy also as she danced with him.

Was Nana right? Did Nick have feelings for her too? Did she really even want that?

"Are you hungry, Nick," Jill asked still locking eyes with him.

"More hungry than you can ever know," he responded with fire in his gaze.

"You don't mean food, do you Nick?" She asked wetting her lips with her tongue.

"No, I don't," and he pulled her to him.

She slowly raised her arms and draped them around his neck drawing herself even closer. They were a perfect fit. She heard him issue a small gasp and then he responded by claiming her lips with more force than he had intended but she met him with equal strength. She pulled back slightly, still locked in his gaze. She took his hand and led him across the hall to her quarters never taking her eyes off his.

Nick wasn't sure where this was going but allowed himself to be drawn along by her. He had never been in her place. She led him to an oversized sofa, threw off a couple of pillows and pulled him down with her.

The kisses were deep and hot and Jill thought she would lose her mind. She had never had these sensations in her life. Certainly not with Geoffrey. She pulled back and unbuttoned a few of the buttons of his shirt running her hands over his chest.

The sensations pouring through Nick made him feel like he was drowning. But he didn't want to come up for air. She started giving him softer, sexier kisses over his face and neck. Slowly she changed her position so that she was sitting more on top of him. They kept their eyes locked and Nick undid the rest of the buttons of his shirt and Jill ran her hands across his chest and abdomen, kissing the base of his throat as she did so.

Nick started to groan. He was as breathless as she. God help him, but he wasn't sure he could stop. He was so in love with her. *Lord, please give me the strength I need to not compromise this woman.*

She sat up and pulled her tee shirt over her head tossing it behind the sofa keeping her eyes on him as she did. She had never behaved this way in her life. Never even thought of it. She was on fire for this man. Her concerns about being too heavy for him had gone out the window.

Nick tried so hard not to look at her but she was so well built and that lacy bra… no padding. It was all her. He had wondered.

He moved so that she was sitting on his lap and he heard her gasp. He ran both his hands down her arms causing goose bumps all over her body. He could see the effect he was having on her and he thought to himself, *I'm about to cross a line here and I won't be able to take it back. I already have one daughter out of wedlock.* These thoughts moved fleetingly through his mind.

Jill locked her fingers with his and asked again. "Are you hungry Nick?"

"So hungry," he replied barely able to get the words out.

"Do you want to eat, Nick?"

"Yes, so bad, you have no idea."

"I think I have some idea," she teased him and his face flamed bright red.

Jill leaned in closer to him and whispered, "What would you like to eat, Nick?"

Man, she was so hot! He couldn't help it, his eyes strayed to her breasts and she noticed. She reached behind her to undo her bra when…

"Dad! Have you eaten yet?" Anika yelled through the door.

Nick felt like he had been doused with ice cold water. Jill jumped up grateful she didn't get the chance to unhook her bra and dived over the end of the sofa. She grabbed her tee shirt and hastily threw it on.

Nick grabbed Jill's wrist and pulled her to him. "No honey," he answered Anika. "I didn't get to eat. I'll be down in a minute."

"Okay, I'll save something for you." And they heard her run down the stairs.

Jill was as red in the face as he was and she started buttoning his shirt.

"I am so sorry Nick. I've never done anything like that in my life. If Anika hadn't come up here…well, I may not have stopped."

"And I may not have had the strength to stop either. Okay, deep breath, deep breath," said Nick rubbing his eyes.

"Jill, I just have to say, you are the most beautiful, sexy, totally hot female I have ever encountered."

He hesitated looking away for a minute wondering if he was revealing too much of his heart too soon.

"I think I may be falling in love with you."

Jill wasn't sure how to respond. *Did she follow Nana's advice and just be Jill? Was she just being Jill a minute ago?*

"Nick, I feel the same way about you but we come from such different places in society. How do we deal with that?"

"I think I fit quite well in your life here in West Virginia and I know you'll fit quite well in mine in New York City," he answered.

"I guess we'll find out soon enough," she said.

"I need to hear you say it too, Jill, please."

"You know my story, so you have to know how hard I tried not to, but I am so in love with you, Nick. So much, it hurts."

"Thank you," was all he said and pulled her in for a soft kiss.

As they went downstairs for dinner, they passed Nana at the bottom of the stairs. All she did was wink and kept on going.

~

They arrived at the airport at nine the next morning having been driven by an animated Josie. Anika and Matt were just as talkative about what was to take place in the next few days. Jill headed for the terminal entrance saying they had better get their luggage checked and see if the flight was on time.

"No need," said Nick. "Our pilot is here and waiting."

"Say what?" Matt looked around. "Aren't we on a commercial flight?"

"For a forty-five-minute trip? I think not," said Nick opening the door for Jill. "Rod will fly us."

Just then Rod came around the corner dressed in casual clothing and sunglasses. He took the glasses off and asked if everyone was ready to hit the skies.

Josie was the first to speak. "Rod Wallace, I've picked you and Gwen up here a couple of times and you never mentioned to me that you had flown yourself! You're a pilot!" She stated the obvious. "Why didn't you tell me?"

"I didn't think about it," he said offhandedly.

"Don't feel bad, Josie. I'm his niece and I didn't know it either," groused Anika.

They all looked at Nick. "Hey! Chill! I didn't find out about it until last weekend myself." Jill was just shaking her head.

"Well, are you all ready? The jet is fueled up and ready to go," said Rod.

They all looked at each other. Finally Nick said. "Jet? Seriously? You didn't tell me you owned a jet!"

"I didn't think about it," Rod repeated.

He led them through the terminal and out a side door. The small private jet was beautiful. Josie wanted to look inside and see the cockpit. After she was satisfied that the jet was safe, she looked Rod in the eye.

"You take care of my family. This is very precious cargo."

"Hey, what about Anika and I?" Nick smiled as he teased her.

"Y'all are family too," she said as she was starting to tear up. She gave Rod a hug, and then hugged the rest in turn before she left.

"Rod, you call me as soon as you're on the ground, you hear me?" She was yelling as she headed for the terminal.

Jill felt the thrust as Rod smoothly guided the jet into the air. She looked at the others and Anika looked, for a moment, like she was going to be sick.

The flight was quick and smooth, proving Rod to be an excellent pilot. Matt had sat in the cockpit and was full of questions. Rod was very patient with him and even gave a little instruction at times.

The landing was as smooth as glass and Nick was very impressed with his little brother. As they departed, Rod told Nick he would be flying the rest of the family up on Saturday in time for the concert and banquet. A limo was waiting and took them to the Grand Wallace New York.

As they left the limo, they were met by Oscar, the doorman.

"Nicolai! My main man!" He greeted Nick with a quick handshake. "I thought I'd never see you again after you left that last time! How have you been, my brother?"

They made small talk and Nick introduced everyone, with Anika getting a big hug from Oscar. He helped them with their bags and ushered them up to Nick's suite.

"Wow! What a place, dude!" said Jill looking around.

"Still going with 'dude' are we?" Nick cocked his head to the side and was looking her in the eye.

"Okay, how about 'what a place, you sexy hunk of manhood," said Jill grabbing the front of Nick's shirt as she flirted with him.

Anika was appalled. "Yuck!" She put her hands over her ears and started loudly singing 'God Bless America' to drown out anything else they might say.

"Stop it Annie," Matt said laughing. "Show me your room."

Nick stepped in saying, "Anika, you know I don't usually allow boys in your room, so no shenanigans."

"Did it stop you?" She had nailed him. He saw Jill's face, and they were both thinking the same thing. *Had she been listening outside the door?* God, he hoped not. Anika was too intuitive for her own good!

Jill tried to cover her embarrassment by addressing Nick.

"Where should I put my things?"

"My room?" Nick was being playful.

"Come on, be serious," she said.

"Who said I wasn't?" He pointed towards a room on the other side of the suite. She punched his arm and went in the direction he pointed just as a knock sounded at the door. He answered it to find his mother on the other side.

"Hello mother," he said in his most formal tone. "To what do I owe this...he couldn't say pleasure, so he went with 'visit'."

"I just wanted to see if you would really have the nerve to bring that hillbilly lot into this domain." His mother stood as stiff as possible with her nose in the air.

"Nice to see you too," said Nick as he stepped out into the hall closing the door before Matt or Jill heard her tirade.

"And where, pray tell, is your father?" she continued.

Nick was doing all he could to hold his tongue. "Pappy," he said rubbing it in, "didn't come with us. He will fly in on Saturday with Rod."

"Rod who?" She looked very confused. "And who is this 'pappy'? Some grubby old vagrant you've unwittingly given charity to?"

"It makes me really sad to have to answer these questions, mother. Rod is your son and pappy is your husband," stated Nick with much emphasis on 'son' and 'pappy' as he could muster.

"Oh my God!" She was livid. "He's crossed over! I was afraid of that. I should have done more to keep him from going!"

"Rod, your son, anything to say about him?"

"I guess a pilot is admirable. That could be of some use to the company. Does he have his own plane?"

"He owns a jet." Nick was starting to feel a headache coming on.

"That's even better. Perhaps I should have a meeting with him," she said tapping her finger to her cheek while she was thinking.

"Your own son, but then again, what did I expect from you, mother? Caring, concern? I have had enough of this conversation." Nick moved to go back inside his room when she grabbed his arm to stop him.

"Do I get to meet...what's the word? Entourage just doesn't seem to fit these people," she said. "Do I get to meet your... posse?"

"Not if I can help it," said Nick. "And while you're at it, take off those stupid gloves. You've been wearing them since I was born!"

Nick opened the door, went through it, and slammed it in her face. It felt good! When he turned around, Jill was standing there.

"Sounds like a lovely woman," she said sarcastically. She was also trying hard not to laugh at the look on Nick's face.

"She didn't even know the name of her last-born son. That is pathetic!" Nick tried to rein in his emotions.

"Rod even grew up in the same penthouse as she and dad. What does that say about Gerard? He grew up in England. She's most likely forgotten all about him." Nick started to pace when another knock sounded on the door.

"She had better not be back," said Nick jerking the door open. It was Gwen.

"I figured you were here since I passed mother in the hall and she was seething," said Gwen. "Is father with you?"

Nick explained that the others would arrive on Saturday and that father now preferred to be called 'pappy'.

"You're kidding!" Jill and Nick filled her in on what had transpired since her last visit. After digesting some of the new information she had been given, Gwen turned to her 'all business' mode.

"You have a practice scheduled with the symphony at two this afternoon," she said handing him an itinerary.

"I'll take Matt with me. I need to let the orchestra know about the two new pieces of music to be performed," said Nick as he ran down the list Gwen had given him.

"Were you able to get a nice song together for Alphonse?" she asked.

Nick looked at his sister with a smirk on his face. "I got a song together but I can't say it's all that nice. It's a variation of 'Twinkle, Twinkle, Little Star'."

"You didn't! That's sheer genius! It fits him perfectly!" Gwen was gushing with excitement. "It's going to really yank his chain!"

"I can't wait to meet this guy," said Jill glancing at Nick's list and brushing up against his arm while she did. "Not!"

Gwen looked from Jill to Nick and raised her eyebrows but seemed to decide against whatever question was on her mind.

"You'll get to meet Alphonse soon enough. While Nick is at practice, I've arranged for you to do your time watching his cooking demonstration."

"Might as well get it over with," said Jill despondently.

"What am I supposed to do while you all are tied up?" Anika was whining again.

"Your grandmother has demanded to spend a little time with you. Says she has a gift she thinks you will like. That's all I know about it," said Gwen.

"No!" wailed Anika. "Can't I stay with you?"

She was tearing up quickly and glancing around for Matt who was looking out the picture window, ignoring them all.

"Sweetheart, I have to be at the symphony practice or I would love to spend the afternoon with you, you know that," said Gwen putting her arm around Anika trying to console her.

"Why do you have to be at the practice?" Anika continued to whine.

"Because I play with the symphony orchestra."

"What?" Nick was stunned. "When did this happen? I didn't even know you played an instrument. What do you play?"

"Skeleton time again," said Jill giving him a hug.

"I play the flute," she stated. "I also have played on three of your concerts and you never even noticed me. Even when I went up and said 'hello' to you."

"Well, that's just great!" Nick was obviously embarrassed. "This family is more screwed up than I thought. I'm so sorry, Gwen. I have been in my own little world for so long. I'm as bad as mother."

"No one is that bad. Now, let's get some lunch and get this piece of the trip over with." Gwen led them out the door toward the elevators.

Gwen and the kids took one elevator and Nick waited with Jill for the other.

Jill looked at Nick. "Does Anika ever ask about her mother? She's here in New York isn't she?"

"We've discussed it and she seems to have a good grip on it, or so she says. She feels like if her mother didn't want her, at least she did the right thing by leaving her with me and Aunt Bess. She says she understands that Erica was a child and I let her think that Erica did the best she could at the time. If she ever wants to meet her, I can arrange it."

"Do you ever see her, Nick?" Jill asked fearing the answer.

"No. I've never wanted to and since I met you, I'll never be able to look at another woman. Ever."

As the elevator doors closed, he pulled Jill to him and proceeded to show her just how much he meant that.

Sixteen

They parted ways after they had eaten lunch in one of the hotel's bistros. Oscar had volunteered to take Jill to meet Alphonse and he led her to the back entrance to the kitchen. He explained that Alphonse was under a lot of pressure today due to the arrival of twenty high ranking government officials that would be dinning later in the day.

Wonderful, thought Jill, but she was kind of looking forward to seeing how well a New York French kitchen was run.

"I'm sorry Miss Jill to have to leave you in the presence of this …how should I put it? Unsavory character, but I have to get back to my post. Oh, and try not to laugh when you meet him," said Oscar.

Jill pulled out her cell phone and was trying to look for a picture saying, "I saw him on the internet. He was very good looking."

"It's a matter of opinion, you'll see." Oscar knocked on the door before sticking his head in and saying a few words to someone on the other side. After the brief conversation, he tipped his hat to Jill and left.

After a couple more minutes, the door opened and out strutted Alphonse Laurant. All five feet, four inches of him.

Jill had to look down to see him and she clamped her lips shut, tight.

Alphonse walked slowly around her, looking her up and down and lingering in areas he shouldn't. He reminded Jill of a bantam rooster strutting around the chicken coop trying to attract the hens.

"So, we finally meet," he said in his genuine French accent.

"So it seems," said Jill.

He continued to look at her, even bent over to get a better look at her legs. *What a creep*, she thought.

"You're not what I thought," he said, eyes returning to her chest, but if she were to be fair, at his height, that might have been his natural line of vision.

"You look nothing like you do on the internet."

"Ditto," said Jill.

"You are quite pretty to look at. Are you sure you are the real Mountain Mama and not some imposter?"

Jill switched to Mountain Mama mode. "Yer a lookin' at the real thing, sure as shootin' ye are."

"Please, please! My delicate ears! That does it. You shall not date me. Not now, not ever!" He strutted back into the kitchen motioning for her to follow.

"Aw, shucks! You done gone an' broke my heart. What'll I do! The shame of it all." Jill hammed it up.

"All the girls want Alphonse. I am sure you are no different. Maybe if you show me some more skin, I will reconsider."

Alphonse moved his finger like he was going to lift her skirt.

"In your dreams, sucker. And if you move that finger any closer, I will personally cut it off and shove it up… where the sun don't shine!" She stepped closer to him and he backed away.

"Enough of this nonsense, woman. Stand off to the side and watch a real master chef in action," he said loud enough for all the workers to hear. "I have many dishes to prepare in a short period of time and I don't need you in the way."

"Hey, dude, this was all your idea, not mine." But she backed slightly off and prepared to see if she could tell who was doing what. It looked like a royal mess to her. Pure chaos all over the kitchen.

She observed for a while and noticed how unhappy the kitchen crew seemed to be. She could not tell who were the chefs and who were the dish washers. All were treated equally horrible. Alphonse gave no direction but yelled at everyone and at times dumped the food out on the floor stating it wasn't fit for a dog to eat.

As she watched him cook, she tried to point out some ways he could improve his technique and save some time. He turned on her and started cursing and stamping his feet.

"Who do you think you are to tell me how to cook food from my native land? You could never measure up to the great Alphonse! You are nothing compared to me."

He kept hitting the side of a cabinet to emphasize each word. Jill looked up to see a large, heavy looking pot, teetering on the edge ready to fall. She spoke up to warn him but Alphonse screamed at her.

"Silence!" As he did, he punched the cabinet with his fist.

The pot started to fall and Alphonse looked up just as the pot landed on his head with a resounding 'crack'. He hit the floor and was out, cold.

Jill looked up. "Call 911!" Everyone just stopped what they were doing and stared. She realized no one wanted to help this man so she whipped out her cell phone and called herself.

One of the workers came over with a wet washcloth and started wiping blood off Alphonse's head. Jill felt his pulse and it was strong and steady.

"We can't get this food prep done without him," the man said in a French accent.

"Where are your Sous Chefs?" she asked.

"I am a Sous Chef, but Alphonse never lets us take the lead," the man continued.

"It is a mess back here. He yells and screams at everyone. The turnover is ridiculous and not everyone here speaks English. He gives most of his instructions in French."

"Here come the paramedics," said Jill. They quickly assessed the situation and were quick to get Alphonse onto the gurney and into the ambulance.

"What is your name?" Jill turned to the man that had helped.

"Henri." And he gave the names of the others that were gathered around.

"Mrs. Wallace will be very upset when she hears of this. We will not be ready when the officials arrive."

"Well then, let's get started and finish up this food prep. Tell me what has been done and what needs to be done."

Jill took charge giving instructions in fluent French to the surprise of all. She grabbed an apron and they all began to work together. While they were working, she heard more horror stories about working with Alphonse.

"Why do they let him keep running this place?" she asked.

"Well now, that is the question of the hour, isn't it?" said Henri.

They had all the food prepared by the time the officials started to arrive. Jill thanked everyone, continuing to speak in French and told them how much she had enjoyed working with them. Jill turned around to find a petite older woman watching her from just inside the doorway. She was barely five feet tall with short spiky gray hair, enough makeup for several people, and obvious plastic surgery. Lot of plastic surgery, so much so that the woman's whole face looked plastic. She was wearing an expensive looking suit and elbow length gloves. This must be Nick's mother.

She moved forward and stated formally.

"Margaret Wallace," and she held out her hand. Jill took it.

"Jill Dennison, nice to make your acquaintance."

"Yes," said Margaret. "I am impressed with your French and the way you have this kitchen running so smoothly. It rarely runs this well."

"Thank you. I was just here to observe Alphonse for the afternoon but when he had his accident, as a chef myself, it was my duty to help out," Jill responded.

"You will be compensated for your trouble," stated Margaret in an authoritative voice.

"That's not necessary," said Jill, "but I would like to speak with you about a few things I observed that you could change to make things run a little smoother."

They retreated to an office area at the back of the kitchen. Jill had insisted that Henri join them as well.

As they talked, compliments and requests to meet the chef were pouring in from the officials and others present in the restaurant. Margaret ushered Jill to the dining area and she pulled Henri along with her since he had done a good majority of the cooking.

They spoke with several of the officials and retreated to a more secluded table with a great view away from the main dining area.

That was where Nick and Gwen found Jill, seated at a table talking and laughing with his mother and Henri.

Before approaching, Nick stopped one of the kitchen workers and asked what was going on. He received a rundown of the afternoon's events surrounding Alphonse's accident. Gwen took off for the hospital to see about Alphonse's health while calling her father and Gerard to do damage control.

Matt and Anika had found Nick and they all approached his mother's table with caution.

"Hello, again, mother."

Henri stood to shake Nick's hand giving his apologies so he could get back to the kitchen. Nick took his seat and the kids went to look at the view of New York out of earshot of the coming conversation.

"Nicolai, I'd like you to meet Jill. She just saved the day by organizing and helping to prepare the food for the government officials this afternoon. She's also made several suggestions for improving the running of the kitchen that will be time saving and cost effective in the long run." His mother was almost gushing with her praise.

"That's great news mother," said Nick with a hint of sarcasm. "And I'd like you and your gloves to also meet Jill, my girlfriend as well as owner and chef of Mountain Mama's restaurant in Beaumont, West Virginia.

His mother's face was white with shock as she stood and faced Jill.

"How dare you deceive me like this! Nicolai, are you behind this?"

"No, I am not, but why the change of attitude? I just heard all the compliments you had for Jill. The kitchen staff says she really pulled through for this place," said Nick.

His mother composed herself and looked at Jill.

"I apologize for my outburst. Thank you again for stepping in, but as I have no respect for the state of West Virginia or the people in it, I would thank you in the future to ask my permission before you just help yourself to someone else's territory!" She turned and stalked off with a haughtiness that would have made Gerard proud.

Seventeen

"What a piece of work!" Matt stated out loud as he watched her retreat.

"No kidding," said Jill looking wary.

"I am so sorry," said Nick. "There is no excuse for her but let's not let that ruin the rest of our evening.

"Don't worry about it. She and I were getting along famously before she found out where I live," said Jill. "I've had to face that kind of prejudice before. In this case, I feel like we're missing a piece of the puzzle, though."

"I am sure we are," said Nick. "I plan to have a nice talk with dad about where all of this is going as soon as we get back home."

"Did you hear yourself?" asked Jill.

"What did I say?"

"You referred to West Virginia as 'home'."

"Babe, home is where the heart is and my heart is where ever you are." Nick pulled her to him for a kiss.

Anika mimed throwing up.

"Yeah, I'm with you on that one, Annie," said Matt looking disgusted.

Just then, Henri returned to their table with an apron signed by all the kitchen staff. He bowed low and kissed her hand as he spoke to her in French thanking her again. She answered him in French which was a surprise to Nick and Anika.

"I didn't know you spoke French!" Anika was awestruck.

"I do okay, it's a little rusty but you have to remember I studied in France. Italy and Japan also. I have a working knowledge of those as well, but I studied French in school."

"Dad speaks German and Dutch and so do I," said Anika. "Come to think of it, so does Grampy."

"Grampy?" Jill and Nick said together.

"He said I could call him whatever I want, and that's what I chose," she defended herself.

"So what does that make your grandmother?"

"I plan to call her Granny."

"Anika, honey, I'll give you a thousand dollars if you let me tell her," said Nick sounding serious.

Jill kicked him under the table but she was laughing.

"So, dad speaks German and Dutch too. Must be why he insisted I speak it and he must have had you learn it while you were living there. Is that right, Anika?"

"Yep. He used to drill me on the words and the dialect. One time he put on a straw hat and sang some song that he said was an old Amish song. It sounded like a combination of German and Dutch and grandmother threw a fit. She started cutting up the hat with some scissors. That was a bad fight. I got out of there quick and ran to Gwen's place. She told me that sometimes her father did things like that." Anika started doodling on a napkin.

Matt sensed the subject was getting too heavy for Anika so he tried to lighten the mood.

"I speak German too. Also, a little Italian and a tiny bit of French that I learned listening to Nick on the internet!"

He knew well enough to duck quick before Jill clobbered him and maybe Nick might clobber him too.

They played around speaking in different languages until Nick's phone rang. Gwen was calling to let them all know that Alphonse was going to be okay. He had a mild concussion and had been diagnosed with high blood pressure.

"He'll have to go on medication. I spoke with dad and he says now we have a reason for the banquet. 'Injured in the line of duty'. He thinks he's funny these days."

Alphonse would be discharged from the hospital the next day but would not be allowed to return to work until next week. Nick put Henri in charge of the kitchen and they went to brief the staff.

Matt told Jill and Anika how the practice had gone. He was so excited.

"I met so many unbelievably talented musicians. I was nearly overwhelmed. They're doing a couple of songs on the concert that I've done before and the director, Dr. Richard Dana, is going to let me sit in on those."

"At least you had a better time than I did," said Anika. "Grandmother was a nightmare! The gift she had for me was a million dollars to come back to New York permanently and bring grandfather with me. I told her flat out 'no'. She got really mad and called me an ungrateful wench. I just said 'whatever' and left."

Nick returned from the kitchen and told them everything was set and that he had obtained tickets for a Broadway show later in the evening. They all returned to Nick's suite to change and get ready for dinner before the show.

They ate at a trendy upscale restaurant where the food was very good. *Not as good as Jill's* thought Nick. He had heard from the kitchen staff what a jerk Alphonse had been to her. Henri couldn't say enough good about how she handled everything.

"Babe, I am so proud of you. I told you how well you would fit right in."

"I had fun. I haven't done French cuisine in a while, but I still had fun," she said.

"I'm glad." She felt him give her knee a squeeze under the table.

"How about tomorrow I take Anika and you take Matt so we can do shopping and, you know, guy and girl stuff."

"Makes the most sense," said Nick. "How about we shop until about two in the afternoon, eat, and go on a tour of Julliard. We can hit some other spots as well. Any place you want to go."

"Sounds fun," said Matt and Anika agreed.

"Dad, how about tomorrow morning Matt and I could go sight- seeing by ourselves and you and Jill can have some time alone too," said Anika hopefully.

"Sounds good to me," said Nick. "If it's okay with you, Jill. Anika knows her way around so they should be fine."

Jill agreed and since that was settled, they made their way to the theater. Nick watched Jill as she took in the sights and sounds of New York City on their short walk to the theater. She was graceful as she walked and had a nice, sexy swing to her hips.

As his mind started to go south, he noticed that Matt seemed to be watching Anika in the same way. He had trusted Matt with Anika, but not sure he trusted Anika with Matt. She could be very persuasive. When he was Matt's age, he had already been a father for two years, so maybe it was time for a heart to heart talk with Matt after they were back from this trip.

~

It was after midnight when they returned to Nick's suite. The kids went to their rooms while Nick and Jill sat in the dining area.

"Would you like some coffee?" asked Nick.

"I don't drink coffee," said Jill. "I prefer pop or tea."

"Me too," said Nick. "I just keep it on hand for guests that ask for it. So, what did you think of the show?"

"I thought It was very well done and that lead actress was phenomenal the way she played her part," said Jill. "I was reading in the program that she had been nominated for a Tony award."

"She was good," said Nick and he became very silent resting his head on the back of the love seat they were sitting on.

"What's wrong? You look upset," asked Jill.

"Not upset, but not sure how to say this or what to do about it."

"Uh, oh," said Jill. "Out with it."

"I asked Oscar to get me some tickets for a current Broadway play that had good reviews," said Nick.

"I had no idea who was in it until we sat down and the play began. I double checked the program to be sure. The lead actress was Erica Baymore, Anika's mother." Nick watched Jill to gauge her reaction.

"I see," she said. "She's beautiful. Does Anika know?"

"No, she's never really asked her mother's name. Well, she knows it's Erica and that she lives in New York. I have not given her any further information. I figure when she wants to know, she'll ask."

They sat in silence for a while, each with their own thoughts. Finally, she said she was really tired, gave him a kiss on the cheek and went to her room.

Nick wondered if she felt intimidated by Erica. She shouldn't. Erica could never outshine Jill in his mind. He kept dwelling on how loveable Jill always looked. She was well dressed, articulate, poised, and that sexy walk of hers.

He smiled to himself. He wanted a real kiss, not the peck on the cheek.

He knocked softly on her door hoping he wasn't waking her. She answered dressed in the cutest little pair of flimsy shorts and tee shirt top. He was sure it wasn't sold to entice the opposite sex but on her, it was very enticing.

"I didn't want to go to sleep until I got a real kiss."

He was trying to keep his eyes on her face but failing miserably. Especially when she stretched her arms over her head. He bet she did that just to tease him.

Jill opened the door and pulled him inside. She couldn't decide if it would look less suspicious if the door remained open or if it was closed. She knew how this would look if one of the kids decided to get back up.

"So you want a kiss? Is that all?" she asked.

"Jill, baby, don't tempt me like that. My will power is at an all-time low, but I love you so much."

"If it's a kiss you want, then a kiss is what you shall have. I'll do the kissing, you stand still."

She stood a little on her tip toes and licked his bottom lip with her tongue, then kissed his chin, eyes, and ears, leading each kiss with her tongue, all the while whispering of her love for him.

He couldn't stand it. He was so enticed he felt like he would pee his pants. He grabbed her shoulders and pulled her to him and claimed her lips. His need was great.

"Babe, I want you". Nick ran his hand through her hair.

"I want to drink in all of you, kiss all of you, and wake up next to you." He could tell she had nothing on under the pajamas. He was about to put his hand where he knew he shouldn't when...

"Sis, can I talk to you for a minute?" Matt softly knocked the door.

Nick cursed and jumped backwards hitting the closet door in the process.

"What do we do now?" he asked.

"Okay, let me think." Jill stepped away to grab a robe and stepped onto the spike of one of her heels and she cried out.

"Sis are you okay? What's going on? It sounds like you're hurt. Wait, I'll go get Nick," said Matt.

"No wait," she said. She opened the door a crack. "What is it? Can't it wait until morning?"

"No, I just came from Anika's room and that girl is so hot I still haven't been able to catch my breath." They could hear heavy breathing.

"What?" Nick threw the door wide open.

Matt was doubled over laughing and pointing at them. He really couldn't catch his breath. Jill and Nick were both red faced but thankfully, still dressed.

"I heard you talking about Anika's mother and when I came out, I saw Nick knock on your door, sis. I'm sorry. It was too good an opportunity to miss. And I wasn't in Anika's room. I know better, unlike some in this room." He was still laughing.

Nick felt he owed Matt one.

"When you get hot and bothered by the female gender, young man, you need to take a cold shower and cool down."

He grabbed Matt by the shirt front and dragged him laughing into the bathroom and shoved him in the shower. He turned on the cold water just as Matt pulled Nick under the cold spray as well.

"Hey, no fair," cried Nick trying to turn off the water.

"Yes, fair," laughed Matt. "I'm not the one who needs the cold shower." Matt turned the water off and they both sank down to sit in the shower, both laughing, totally soaked.

Jill stood in the living room, not knowing what to say. She finally turned on her heel.

"Good night," she said and went back to her room and shut the door.

The next morning Jill was up early. She hadn't slept well what with the close call again with Nick last night. She had also been thinking about Erica Baymore and the fact that if Nick wanted to pursue a relationship with her, then she could never compete with that.

She showered and dressed for chilly weather with easy to remove clothing for their shopping trip. She knew they would be in and out of dressing rooms most of the day. She went into the main area of the suite and found Nick and a waiter arranging food on a buffet cart.

"Good morning, babe," he said. "Beautiful as ever, I see."

He walked over to her for a kiss which she was happy to provide.

"It was so hard to sleep after last night's encounter."

Jill started kissing him playfully all over the face, when he pulled her down onto his lap and deepened the kiss. Matt and Anika walked in and interrupted, of course.

"You two should see yourselves. It's disgusting," said Anika. "Look, this is you." She grabbed a laughing Matt and pulled him closer.

"Oh honey, oh baby, you're the bomb. Let me kiss you all over until we explode!" She started kissing Matt all over the face with exaggerated kissing sounds.

Matt caught the drift and grabbed her by the shoulders. "Oh, you horny woman! Come make my day, my minute, my hour!"

He swung Anika backwards in a dip and pretended to kiss her with passion, although maybe he wasn't pretending.

"Okay, Okay, you two. We get the picture," said Jill. "Now, get yourselves some breakfast so we can get going."

They ate and went off in pairs. Anika and Jill went to several exclusive shops until they found the perfect gowns and accessories. They spent some time having their nails done and toenails as well, all the while talking about 'girl stuff'. Jill realized she was coming to love this young girl very much.

Matt and Nick each had been fitted for a tux and Nick bought them both instead of just renting them. He told Matt that it never hurt to have a nice tux in the closet for special occasions. He had really wanted to do this for the boy.

They both got haircuts and Matt had his longish style hair cut short, similar to Nick's. Nick treated Matt to some other fashionable clothing that he could wear to school. Nick felt he had really bonded with the boy and took great pains to try to explain about his relationship with Matt's sister and how much he loved her.

They all met for lunch and talked about their mornings adventures in finding formal wear. They all had funny stories to tell and as they ate and laughed, Nick realized what a nice family they appeared to be and he wished he could hold on to this moment forever.

Eighteen

Gwen joined them for breakfast the next morning in Nick's suite. She was updating them about how well Alphonse was doing and about the throngs of women trying to get to him at the hospital.

"It's really disgusting! I go into his room and two are in the bed next to him and three others arguing over who gets to be next. I can't figure out what any decent woman sees in him."

"I think 'decent' may be the key word here," said Nick. "I don't think any decent woman would, but I don't think decent women are his style."

Matt put his two cents in. "It's money and power. It seems that he portrays himself to have both of these things. I have no idea how much money he has, but he does have notoriety as the chef of the famous Marcel's."

Nick changed the subject and informed Gwen of the morning's plans and that Rod would be flying Josie, Lance and Andrew in later in the day. Gerard would be flying commercial and they would all meet for lunch at Marcel's around two in the afternoon.

Jill had spoken with her mother, and Nana was under the weather again so she would be staying behind to take care of her. Her father had elected to stay behind as well to help out in the restaurant.

Gwen informed them that after lunch, she had booked all the 'girls' for a spa treatment and makeover that would take several hours, almost until concert time.

Anika grabbed Jill's hand and almost squealed.

"I can't wait! Thank you, Aunt Gwen!"

Later in the afternoon, everyone was seated around a table at Marcel's. Henri had done himself proud with a magnificent lunch that could have rivaled Alphonse.

"It was so thrilling!" Josie was practically gushing. "The view from the cockpit is unbelievable!"

"Tell me about it," said Matt. "There's no other way to travel, no other way."

Gerard had been silent listening to the conversation so far and looking from Josie to Matt.

"So how is it that you two managed to get to ride in the cockpit of a plane? What kind of a professional airline allows that?"

"Rod's airline," said Rod.

"What airline is that? Some hillbilly crop duster you paid with a couple of chickens and a bottle of moonshine?" Gerard said in his snotty way.

"No, you jerk," said Rod. "I flew these guys here myself, and if you had bothered to try to get to know any of us, like Nick and I have, you would have known that."

"You," said Gerard pointing at Rod with a smirk on his face, "have a plane?"

"Jet," said Josie. "He owns a jet and it is beautiful. And he is an excellent pilot. So I would thank you to keep your nose back on your face where it belongs. And keep your fly trap shut. Especially if you have no idea what you're talking about."

"A jet? Yeah, right. That'll be the day."

"Son, I don't know what your problem is, but you have no reason to doubt your brother. All of us have flown with him. And he really does own a jet," stated Andrew a little louder than he had meant.

"And a helicopter," said Rod.

"What!?" They all said in unison.

"You are just full of surprises today," said Josie.

"Well," said Gerard. "I want to see this jet. Why didn't you tell me?

"I didn't think about it," said Rod. "The subject never came up."

Gwen started to get up, and gather the girls for the spa appointment. "Let's go, girls. I've had enough of Gerard's mouth for today."

"How about us guys go show the jet to Gerard. I want to get out of here before I run into your mother. Tonight is soon enough for me," said Andrew.

"Thanks, Gwen for putting me up in your suite so I can avoid her for a while."

"No problem, dad...er...pappy. I don't think I can get used to that anytime soon," said Gwen as she picked up her things and told the girls to follow her.

Jill caught Nick's arm and pulled him to the side. "I'll miss you," she said close to his face.

"Until tonight," Nick answered.

"I won't see you again until after the concert, but understand how much I love you and I'll be counting the hours."

He gathered his nerve, because the family was watching, and pulled her into a kiss.

Matt put his hand over Anika's eyes. "She has a bad reaction to that sort of thing."

Andrew and Gerard just stared. "It appears that we have missed something," said Andrew.

"Come on pappy," said Nick. "I'll fill you all in on the way to see the jet. Keep up, Lance, you'll get to see Gwen later."

Lance sputtered and protested but never got a real word out.

"Nobody here is blind, cuz," said Matt.

The girls had a wonderful time the rest of the evening being pampered in the spa. Jill had never done anything like this and according to Anika, neither had she.

"Grandmother always said I was too young to visit the spa, but I always thought it would help me relax. She kept me so uptight, I sometimes thought I might break into a million pieces."

"Been there, done that," said Gwen in a bored voice.

"I'm just so excited," said Josie. "I can't wait to see Rod all dressed up! He's such a good friend even though

I've only known him for a short time. I give him advice on girls and love. Stuff like that. He's so sweet. He deserves a great girl, but he seems to be a crazy chick magnet."

"I think that runs in the family," said Gwen still in her bored voice.

"No offense, Jill. But look at dad. He has mother and they don't get much crazier than that. And Anika's mother. Who gives up their own child? She had to be crazy. Sorry Anika. I didn't mean to rub your face in it."

"No, it's okay, Aunt Gwen. I made peace with that a long time ago," said Anika a little sadly. "I might want to meet her someday, but not right now."

"You know," said Josie. "My little brother has girls all over him. Remember that one, Ginger, I think her name was. She

used to hang out in front of the house and say she was just passing by."

"Passing by from where? You live out in the boonies. There isn't anything else out there," said Anika.

"Oh, I remember her," said Jill. "She would show up late at night and throw rocks at Matt's window. He had taken her out a couple of times but she was too forward for Matt. Once she tried to climb the trellis in her underwear and dad caught her. She tried to say she was leaving his room but Matt wasn't even home."

"I've got lots of things I can tease him about now," said Anika. "Thanks, ladies!"

Later, back in Nick's suite, Anika and Jill were putting the final touches on their hair and makeup. It was almost time to leave for the concert.

"Jill," said Anika. "Thank you for making this a great trip for me. It wouldn't be the same without you." She was looking at herself in the mirror.

"I don't think I've ever looked this good. I can't wait to see Matt's face."

"Honey," said Jill. "You don't still have a crush on him, do you? Because he tried to make it clear..."

"I know, I know. But yes, I do, how could I not? We're perfect for each other. Maybe if I climb up the trellis in my underwear..."

She ducked when Jill threw a carrot stick at her.

"Hey, don't throw my dinner at me!"

"You're lucky I'm hungry. These vegetables and cheese have to last us through a two hour concert. Are you ready?"

They had taken a limo to the concert hall, all except Nick, Matt, and Gwen who were already there waiting to perform.

~

Andrew finally went to meet with Margaret and escort her to the concert and banquet.

Rod couldn't keep his eyes off Josie. She was dressed in a tea length strapless dress with a gold lace overlay. She seemed to have the same problem keeping her eyes off him, although she would never admit it.

They were ushered into the family's personal seating area, the best seats in the house. Anika and Jill sat together and there was a feeling of excitement all around.

Even when Andrew, Margaret, and a short, balding man entered and took their seats, didn't quite dispel the feeling of magic.

The emcee made a couple of announcements and introduced the symphony orchestra conducted by Dr. Richard Dana, Julliard music professor.

"Next," he continued, "please welcome world-renowned pianist, Nicolai Wallace!"

The audience was on it's feet in an instant as Nick took his place on stage.

Just then, Margaret jumped up and said she had to leave but the balding man insisted she sit back down.

"It's time, Margaret," he said.

Jill would have spent more time wondering what that was about but she remembered that Nick had told her his mother had never been to one of his concerts. *Strange.*

Nick announced from the stage that a few new songs, never before performed, would be performed on the stage tonight.

"The first I'd like to dedicate to a man who is a legend in his own mind... excuse me...in his own right, who was injured on the job yesterday. Alphonse Laurant, please stand."

Alphonse stood from the front row with his usual entourage of women and waved to the audience. He received appropriate applause.

Nick sat and began to play a simple version of 'Twinkle, Twinkle, Little Star' and then the orchestra joined in making the song much more complicated. Nick went into a solo run up and down the piano keys and then a spotlight appeared on the corner of the stage not too far from the piano.

To everyone's surprise, Matt walked out and took his place in the spotlight. He began to play a complicated version of the song on the violin accompanied by the woodwind section.

At the end, the applause was thunderous. Matt took a bow, as did Nick, who also acknowledged the orchestra. Nick could see Dr. Dana trying hard not to laugh at the song that had been dedicated to Alphonse.

Jill was blown away by what Nick and Matt had done with a simple song. For what was meant as a joke, had caused Alphonse to wipe his eyes with his hankie.

Nick spoke into the mic again an announced that the previous song and the coming one, were written by both he and Matt Dennison. He went on to speak a little about Matt and his talent before announcing the next song.

"This song is very special in that I was writing it for my daughter when I found that Matt was also writing a song for her. We pooled our efforts and combined the two for the first piano and violin duet that I have ever performed.

"My daughter, Anika Wallace, this is for you. Anika's Theme. Happy birthday!"

The spotlight landed on Anika and she slowly stood up with tears on her face and blew a kiss to her dad and to Matt before taking her seat again.

Jill had never heard such beautiful music. Anika squeezed her hand through the entire piece. She heard muffled sounds behind her and slightly turned to see Margaret weeping on the balding man's shoulder with Andrew patting her back. *Again, strange.*

After the standing ovation for Anika's Theme, Nick announced that Matt would join the orchestra as the youngest guest player to perform with them in many years. Matt took a bow and went to join the orchestra in the pit.

Nick continued. "This last piece is another special song that I recently wrote for someone else very special in my life. It's not often that a man finds his perfect soul mate, but I have been blessed by her presence in my life and I pray that I will be a blessing in hers. This is for you, Jillian Dennison, with all my love. I hope you enjoy "My Heart for Jill"".

Jill was overwhelmed. That was it, she was a goner. That he would do this for her, she was out of words. This was the most beautiful piece she had ever heard, played solely by Nick on the piano. She found she was grasping Anika's hand just as hard as Anika had hers during Anika's theme. When it ended, Nick stood up and took a bow to a standing ovation. Then he left the stage while the orchestra played a few songs on their own.

Upon Nick's return to the stage, he joined in playing with the orchestra for the rest of the concert. His talent was unequaled anywhere. And as the concert came to an end, she noticed that Nick's parents had left their seats and were nowhere to be seen.

Nineteen

"My dad really loves you, Jill. I can tell," said Anika as they repaired their hair and makeup in the mirror before entering into the main ballroom.

"He loves you very much too Annie, and I can see that on his face every day."

"I know he does. I'm not sure what to think about Matt, though. He went out of his way to write a song for me. Do you think he's changed his mind about how he feels?"

"I don't know, Anika. I guess you are the only one who can determine that. I know the two of you are best friends. Anyone can see that. And there is a certain amount of love that goes into friendship. I'd hate to see that ruined by trying to move into a romantic relationship before either of you is ready."

They made their way to the hall and Jill felt as nervous as Anika about how Nick would react to her formal look. Anika hesitated and told Jill she wanted to talk with Rod and Josie before she entered the hall.

As Jill entered into the main ballroom, she hesitated scanning the room for Nick. Instead she was stopped by Alphonse who was greeting guests as they entered.

"Mountain Mama, you are looking foxy tonight," he said as he ogled her from head to toe.

"You are one of the most beautiful women here. I would also like to apologize for my behavior yesterday. I heard about what you did for me. I thought we had a connection upon our initial meeting and I was proved right, no?"

"No is correct. I did it for the sake of your kitchen staff. For Henri. And for the Wallace's. I would appreciate it if you would stop staring at my..." and she spoke French about what he needed to stop staring.

"Is no matter. I will, now, allow you to date Alphonse. There is no greater honor that I could bestow on you for saving my restaurant."

"I can't date you, Alphonse. I have a boyfriend. Also, and I can't stress this enough, I would rather have a hot poker shoved in my eye than date you!" She turned around to get away from Alphonse and saw Nick standing across the room.

Nick had been talking to his friend and the conductor of the symphony, Dr. Dana, when he noticed Jill enter the room.

"I think this is my cue to exit," said Dr. Dana. "I see the president of the arts society and I had better make the rounds. I will look forward to meeting your friend later in the evening."

Jill was stunning. She had on a slinky, light gray formal gown that was the same color as her eyes. It was held up by spaghetti straps and was flared at the bottom. Her hair had been pinned up to show off her shoulders and neck.

She had diamond like accessories in her hair as well as earrings and a beautiful necklace. He couldn't wait to take her in his arms.

She walked towards him and when they reached each other they shared a lingering kiss. She put her arms around him and whispered how much she loved her song and how much she loved him.

He was resplendent in his tux with the navy-blue accents bringing out the blue of his eyes. A few couples were dancing and Nick moved her onto the dance floor easily and gracefully. They continued to share little kisses and whispering to each other as they barely moved in each other's arms.

When the song ended, they moved to a table on the outskirts of the dance floor. They were joined by Rod and Josie whom Jill had noticed dancing closely when she had been talking with Alphonse.

"Gerard appears to be scoping out the ladies. He seems to be moving around the room stopping to talk to each one," said Matt who had snuck up behind them.

"Look at him. He's kissing the cheek or the hand of each one and it's like they're eating it up. Is he trying to find out which one tastes the best?"

"This is a different side of Gerard," said Rod. "I've never seen him this pleasant before."

"It's probably because he isn't talking to his kin folk. He seems the worst when he's with ya'll," said Josie.

"Speaking of kin folk, Nick, where's your lovely daughter?" asked Matt.

"She was acting like she was afraid to come inside. I think she feels uncomfortable without all that goop she hides behind on her face," said Josie.

"My niece is absolutely the most beautiful girl of her age I have ever seen," stated Rod. "Speaking of which, look, there she is."

Matt stepped forward with his mouth open as if in shock. Anika was dressed in a navy blue halter gown with silver sparkles whenever the light hit her. Her hair was pinned up on one side and cascaded in curls falling onto her opposite shoulder.

Anika saw Matt about the same time he saw her. Her mouth dropped as well. She had rarely seen Matt in anything but flannel or tee shirts. They slowly moved to each other.

"I'm afraid his feelings for her may have changed from friendship."

"I was afraid of that," said Nick. "I will have to have a talk with them, but for tonight, let them have this time together." He nodded to the conductor of the small orchestra and he began music perfect for the Viennese Waltz.

Nick took Jill's hand and swung her onto the dance floor and he saw Matt do the same with Anika. They all moved in harmony across the floor as if they had choreographed this for the entertainment of those present. Most moved away from the dance floor to watch.

Andrew and Margaret entered to see both couples dancing and he led Margaret onto the floor as well.

When the dance was over, Andrew moved towards Nick and Jill.

"May I say, son, you and Jill make a lovely couple, right Margaret?"

"If you say so," she replied barely looking at them.

As the music continued to play, Matt and Anika had slipped from the room. As they walked away from the ballroom for a little privacy Matt took her hand. They had held hands before, but this felt different. Anika drew Matt into the shadows and looked him in the eyes.

"Matt, do you really think I'm pretty? I mean pretty enough without all the makeup I usually wear?"

"Annie, I don't know how to respond to that. I'm breathless. I wanted to write the song for you because you're the best friend I've ever had but my feelings for you are deeperthan that. You are gorgeous, beautiful, I can't even describe how I felt when you walked into the room tonight. I think we'll have to do some more talking but tonight, I just want to be with you, Annie, just you."

"Matt, would you kiss me? I've never really been kissed before. I mean I've had dates, but never a real kiss from the heart. I've always wanted..."

"Annie, you take my breath away." And he slowly lowered his lips to hers.

She put her arms around his neck and Jill happened upon them as Matt was deepening the kiss. She watched for a minute to make sure whether or not she should interrupt. If this was a simple kiss between two good friends she would let it be, but if not...

"Annie, Annie, I...I..."

"I know, Matt, I know," she was out of breath and all of a sudden she jumped up and wrapped her legs around Matt's waist. He started kissing her neck.

Jill recognized passion when she saw it and knew it was time to break them apart before Nick found them.

"Excuse me, Matt, Anika," said Jill. "I think it's time we all had a little talk."

They both jumped apart and Matt was bright red in the face. Anika couldn't look at Jill.

"I'm not sorry," she said.

"Let's go out on the terrace and have a chat before anyone from the family sees the change in you two. Your dad has already started to realize there may be more than meets the eye."

The terrace was enclosed this time of year and except for one other couple, they would be able to freely talk.

"I want you to understand..." Jill started, but Matt interrupted.

"Sis, isn't this the pot calling the kettle, black?"

"Matt, you know it isn't. I'm thirty one and you're eighteen. Anika is not quite seventeen. Think about it for a minute," said Jill as calmly as she could.

"Jill, you act like we were going all the way, and we were just kissing," whined Anika.

"Anika, stop whining. I hate it when you whine," complained Matt.

"Is that right? You didn't hate it a minute ago. Excuse me. I have to get back to the…to the…" and she ran back into the building obviously embarrassed and about to cry.

"Sis, if you don't mind, I'd like to have a minute by myself. I'll be back in soon," said Matt looking at the ground.

"Okay. I'll be in the ballroom if you need me," and she left leaving Matt with his head in his hands.

As she entered the ballroom she saw Nick wave her over to where he was standing with a couple she didn't recognize. Before she could get there, she was stopped at the door by Alphonse again but she was able to shake him off.

She was almost to Nick when she saw Gerard dancing with Erica Baymore. *This can't be good,* she thought. She reached Nick just as he saw them as well.

"I don't believe she's here. What is she up to?" said Nick.

"More than that, what is Gerard doing with her?" asked Jill

"Well, she is a beautiful woman and Gerard is, well, Gerard. I don't know what more needs to be said," remarked Nick with his eyes still on them.

"Yes," said Jill looking at Nick. "You're right. She is beautiful, but could you take your eyes off her for a minute, we might have a situation."

"I'm sorry," said Nick. "What's that supposed to mean?"

Just then a man came up behind Jill and grabbed her, putting his arms around her.

"Hello there, Jillian! I can't believe you are in New York City of all places! Wow! You sure have changed, and may I say for the better!"

"Wonderful! Nick I'd like you to meet Geoffrey Beam," said Jill in a disgusted voice.

"The third," and Geoffrey stuck out his hand to Nick.

Nick briefly shook his hand.

"Nick Wallace," he said looking at Jill.

Jill tried to ignore Geoffrey.

"Nick like I was saying we might have a sit…"

"Excuse me, I was trying to talk to you," interrupted Geoffrey. "I'd appreciate it if you would give me the attention I deserve!"

"You deserve?" Jill put her hands on her hips and pinned him with a stare.

"Why would you think you deserve anything from me? After the way you treated me, I would think you would have had more decency than to barge into a conversation between me and my friend."

"Oh, I see how it is," said Geoffrey. "You're still blaming me for our breakup. If you had tried to be a little better in bed, then I wouldn't have had to seek out other avenues for my pleasure."

Nick heard Jill's sharp intake of breath and felt a great need to defend her.

"I'll have you know that she is great in bed. So hot it'll burn the skin right off your tongue. She can do things you can only dream about. I can barely walk most days, and the nights...let me tell you..."

He had some satisfaction in seeing Geoffrey's face and his astonished look at Jill. But then he saw Matt's. He had heard the whole conversation.

"Is that right, Nick? Sis? Thanks a lot. I need to find Annie since no one else seems to care where she went." Matt left at a jog out of the hall.

"Nick! What were you thinking! Why would you say things like that?"

To Geoffrey she said, "Geoff, if you don't have anything else intelligent to say, please return to your escort and leave me alone!"

"Who told you that Abigail was an escort? That is private information," said Geoff indignantly. Then he softened.

"Jilly, baby, I think you and I should get together for old time's sake." He reached for Jill's arm and she tried to pull away.

Rod noticed the struggle and his brother just standing there. He went over and spoke to Jill.

"May I be of any assistance?" Rod very quietly took his fist and decked Geoffrey Beam the third in the nose.

Taking Josie by the arm, he said, "I think that's our cue to leave."

Jill took Nick's arm and pulled him towards the door and as she looked back, she saw Geoffrey sitting in a chair holding a handkerchief to his bloody nose. *Serves him right*, thought Jill. She was grateful for Rod's help but couldn't help but wonder why Nick didn't step in.

As they exited the door they heard Gerard call them over.

"I'd like you both to meet Erica Baymore. You might recognize her from Broadway or the New York City Ballet.

"Nick," she said. "Long time, no see."

"You know each other?" Gerard was astonished.

"Nick and I go way back," she said sidling over to Nick.

"Gerard and miss, whom ever you are, can Nick and I please have a little privacy? I'm sure you understand." She put her arm around him and gave a little squeeze.

Jill felt like the floor had started to slant and she might have toppled over if not for Gerard.

"Come on, Jill. Let's have at least one dance before the evening is over," and he took her by the hand giving his brother a nasty look.

Jill was hesitant. "Gerard, I don't know. There is a volatile situation going on that could blow up any minute." However, she continued to follow him on to the dance floor anyway.

"Nick, I'm so glad your mother invited me to your concert tonight." Erica continued to touch Nick. To anyone who didn't know them, they must look like lovers having an intimate conversation.

Great! What kind of fresh Hell is this? Nick was ready to jerk his arm loose from hers and find Jill before things got any worse.

"I saw that you dedicated a song to our daughter, and I think maybe it's time for us to consider a relationship again."

"Are you crazy? She is not 'our' daughter. She is 'my' daughter," said Nick who was quickly losing it. "You gave up your right to her almost seventeen years ago. You've never even asked about her since that time. Anika has made peace with that, and if she wants to know more about you, I'll tell her. I'll even arrange a meeting if she wants one, but until that time, *stay away from her!*"

Both were so focused on their intense conversation, neither noticed Anika and Matt standing near them.

Nick looked at Anika and it was obvious that she had been crying. Somewhere in the back of his mind, he remembered Jill trying to tell him about a situation that needed his attention. Nick looked at Erica and gave a slight shake of his head to mean 'no'.

Erica ignored him and walked up to Anika.

"Hello Anika. I'm Erica Baymore, your mother."

Anika faltered but Matt was there to steady her. She backed away from Erica shaking her head.

"What's wrong, dear?" Nick could see the anger flash on Erica's face. "Didn't daddy tell you about me?"

Anika just kept shaking her head and trying to back away but Erica was still advancing. Suddenly, Erica stopped and put her hands on her hips.

"There you go, Nick. There's *your* daughter." She paused.

"You know, when we were kids, I used to regret our little dalliance, but at least, one good thing came out of it."

She paused again and Nick knew she was doing it for dramatic effect. He could also see the tiny flicker of hope in Anika's eyes that her birth mother had feelings for her.

Erica looked Anika straight in the eye.

"I got my education and career financed and my parents are set for life. So go ahead, Nick. Go to your daughter. After all, you bought and paid for her!"

As Erica turned to leave she saw Jill heading their way. Erica quickly went up to Nick and wrapped herself around him, kissing him passionately. She grabbed his hands and pulled them around her so that it looked like they were almost making love up against the wall.

Anika started to cry and ran for the terrace with Matt right behind her.

Jill watched as Erica pulled herself away from Nick and said breathlessly.

"I'm sorry, Nick. No matter how hard you beg, I can't have a relationship with you right now. But since you asked as nicely as you did, of course, I'll spend the night with you. I still remember how good we were together."

Just then, Nick saw Jill's face and it was ready to crumble. However she was able to pull herself together before it did and she followed Anika out to the terrace.

Her heart was breaking but she had to hold it together for Anika's sake. It looked like Nick would be otherwise engaged for the night. She found Anika sobbing so hard she was hyperventilating. Matt was trying to comfort her without any success. Clearly, he was not happy to see Jill.

Finally, Anika was able to choke out a few words.

"I just want to go home!"

"I'll call Rod," said Jill.

He answered in a couple of rings and she explained what had happened. Rod said he was planning on taking Andrew and Josie home tonight and he would take Jill and Anika as well. Jill asked Matt to stay in New York with Nick and Lance to give Anika some breathing room and some for himself, too. Matt reluctantly agreed.

"Let's go get our things and we will meet Rod at the airport," said Jill.

When they emerged into the hallway, Jill saw no sign of Nick nor Erica. She had a queasy feeling in the pit of her stomach, but a little further down the hall, she heard Nick's voice.

"Matt, take Annie to get her things and I will be there in a few minutes."

Jill stopped outside the door to the lounge and heard Margaret voice.

"I invited her because I think it is time the two of you got together. She is a big star and you are famous as well. Anyone can see you're a perfect match. You have got to drop that hillbilly woman now. She'll just hold you back. She's too fat for you and she'll never be good enough for our family."

Jill waited a few minutes to hear what Nick had to say when Andrew came up behind her. He had heard what his wife had said.

"I'm so sorry for what she said, Jill. None of that is true,"

"It's okay, Andy, I've got this!"

Jill had determination on her face. She pushed the door open and walked in with her head held high. She saw Nick turn beet red in the face and he started to run his hands through his hair.

"Family?" Jill paused. "You call what you have, a family? If you want to point fingers, go ahead. You'll have three pointing back at you. You want to call me a hillbilly? Well, I'm proud to be from West Virginia but I can fit into your world just as well and I know you know that. You think I'm fat? Maybe. But I can lose weight. You, however, cannot take back the misery you have caused your precious children and because of your interference in Nick's life here tonight, the misery you have caused your granddaughter! So family? You don't have the first clue! But I'll tell you this. If I ever catch you messing with anyone in my family, or with anyone I have come to think of as family, I will take it out on your sorry hide. And I am not even close to kidding! Have you got that, toots?"

"Yeah! You go girl," hollered Andrew. "Oh, and Margaret, I'm leaving and I won't be returning this time. The next time I see you will be when you seek me out in West Virginia and when the things we have discussed with Dr. Weir have taken place. Until then? Sayonara!"

Andrew started out the door then turned around to address Nick.

"Nick, you'd be a fool to touch that Baymore woman with a twenty foot barge pole."

Jill looked at Nick and he looked back at her. He said nothing so she turned and left with Andrew.

They passed Gerard heading towards the lounge. He saw Margaret standing there with her hand on her chest and a shocked look on her face.

"Hello, mother," said Gerard.

She briefly looked at her son with a question on her face.

"And you are?"

Twenty

Two weeks later, Nick was sitting on his back deck staring out at the Blue Ridge Mountains. It was cold but less so than the last few days. He could see his breath, but the cold didn't bother him. He felt cold all the way through to his heart. He figured if he was that cold all the time, what's a little more. He had been thinking about that last night in New York where everything had gone crazy. How had so many disastrous things gone so wrong, one right after another? There had to be an answer, right? It had been a full moon. He remembered pointing it out to Jill. That was the answer. But he knew in his heart, it was not. He was the real problem.

After the final showdown where Jill had told his mother off and Andrew had told her he was leaving, Nick and Gerard had found Matt and made plans with Rod to fly home the next afternoon.

Matt had manned up and told Nick of the events that took place between himself and Anika. His initial reaction was to do Matt some serious bodily harm but that passed quickly. Who was he to judge.

He had manned up also and explained to Matt that he was making up the things he had said to Geoffrey Beam about Jill.

Matt said that he understood. He would have wanted to defend Jill, as well.

Gerard had been very upset with his mother. Matt, Lance, and Nick had dragged a very drunk Gerard away from the bar in the wee hours of the morning. He had been so drunk, he vomited all over Nick's suite and all over Lance.

Nick and Matt had spent the next day trying to make sense of it all. They had come to some conclusions. Matt should have discussed his changing feelings for Anika with either Nick or Jill. Nick should have been the one to confront Erica as soon as he had seen her instead of hoping she wouldn't see him. And he should have listened to Jill when she had tried to get his attention about what was happening with his daughter. They had prayed together several times and Nick felt the time they'd had was good for both of them.

Rod had flown them home the next afternoon except for Lance. He had stayed a couple more days to observe Alphonse in the kitchen at Marcel's.

Gerard had returned to Philadelphia with Rod to spend a few days getting to know his little brother.

Nick had returned home to find an empty house and a note from Anika that she would be staying with Jill for a while and to please not try to contact her. She needed time to think. Jill had not returned any of his calls so he had decided that they all needed some time apart.

So after two weeks, here he sat, alone on his back deck nearly freezing. If only he could turn back time. Playing the piano was usually cathartic for him, but not this time. He could only seem to play melancholy songs. He missed Jill so much the pain was almost unbearable. He knew he had lost the best thing that had ever happened to him. And his precious daughter...how would he ever repair the damage?

Nick's phone chimed that he had a text coming in.

'Open the door. I'm freezing. Jill'.

He jumped up so fast he knocked over his glass of tea and ran through the house to answer the door.

"Where were you, dude?" Then she thought a little late, that maybe he wasn't alone.

"I'm sorry. I should have called first." She handed him a tabloid newspaper with a picture of he and Erica kissing.

He noticed her looking around and said, "There's no one here but me. I would never bring another woman here. I understand if you don't believe me, but there is no one else. Erica saw you coming and grabbed me. I would never willingly touch that vile woman. And the things she said... she made up. After all she is a Tony winning actress."

"Nick, I understand but I would like to talk to you about a couple of things. We need to sort this out so that we don't have this feeling of misery and discomfort hanging over us and we can move on with our lives," she said.

She was talking of moving on and he knew she didn't mean with him.

"Okay, but I would like to apologize for everything that happened. Jill, I love you whether you believe it or not and that is not going to change. No matter what you have to say. No matter if you meet and start a life with someone else." He braced himself for what she would say.

"Nick, I will always love you too, but this relationship has to end. I can't keep looking over my shoulder for whom ever might come out of your past, be it another woman or your own family. Some of what your mother said was right. I will hold you back. You are the famous Nicolai. You deserve more than I can give. Our worlds are too different. But, if it is possible, I would like to salvage some sort of friendship, for your daughter's sake."

Nick took a deep breath. "Are you sure that is really what you want?"

"Nick, it's what has to be, for all of our sakes," she said with tears in her eyes. "We have to be strong for Annie. She and Matt have had several long talks and they will only be friends from now on. It will be hard for them, but they are strong and have a bond that I think will stand the test of time. Your daughter is amazing. She has done some major growing up."

"Thank you, Jill, for being there for her. Her mother hurt her terribly and I'm hoping that she will be ready soon to sit down and talk about it," said Nick hopefully.

"She will, Nick, but she still needs some time. I'm asking you to trust me here. She's safe with me for now."

"I trust you with my daughter, Jill." He took another deep breath. "So, friends, then?"

"Friends." She held out her hand but he pulled her to him.

"Even friends give hugs," Nick said. "Now go. Please give Annie my love and ask Matt to give me a call or stop by any evening. I have something to discuss with him, if you don't mind."

"I promise on both counts."

Jill left quickly before she lost it altogether. Her broken heart couldn't stand much more. Anika was very distraught because her dad and Jill were not together and this was the only solution she could think of. Anika felt everything was her fault.

"Only a little more than a week until Thanksgiving," said Matt as he sat with Nick at the kitchen table. "Tell me more about this recording session. I'm really stoked!"

"This coming Friday and Saturday, we'll fly to New York and record the new songs we performed on the concert. We'll record Alphonse's song with the orchestra and Anika's theme with just you and I. Then I am going to record 'My Heart For Jill' as well. I've spoken with Jim and Lorraine and they are on board with it. I have another surprise for you that no one knows about yet. Maybe a couple of surprises."

"Man, you're killing me! Don't keep me in suspense!" cried Matt excitedly.

"The conductor of the orchestra, you know, Dr. Dana, would like to extend an invitation for you to join the symphony for the spring season. Between now and then, Rod will periodically fly both of us to New York for rehearsals," said Nick smiling for the first time in several weeks.

Matt just put his head in his hands and thanked the Lord for this opportunity. "I've been so blessed," he said.

"The next order of business, is that I am going to record a new CD and I want you to be a part of that. Maybe Anika as well. We'll work on writing some new music together and I would also like for you to guest on my next concert in February," said Nick feeling some happiness that he was able to give Matt this opportunity.

They ate pizza and talked about how they would start working on new music after the coming recording session was over. Matt was very animated in the discussion until they got around to Anika.

"I am having a very hard time keeping my heart in check," said Matt. "I really do love her and I know we'd be perfect together. I also realize that if we are meant to be together, it will happen in due time. The Lord's time. We just have to pray to be strong and do the right thing when our hearts and carnality are challenged."

"You are one wise young man, Matthew Dennison. Your advice is sound and I would do well to follow it. I feel the same about your sister, as you well know. I will keep praying and wait on the Lord's perfect timing. Thank you," said Nick. "I needed to hear that."

~

Jill sat at a studio table with her Aunts, Shirley, and Gladys going over the ratings and phone calls from the past few weeks. The pilot show with Shirley and Jean had been a huge success and other than the show with Nick, had had more ratings than any other show.

"I'm thinking of taking the show in a new direction," she told them. "I'm thinking of stopping 'Cooking Up A Storm' and

doing the show as myself. Maybe just 'Cooking with Jill' or something like that."

"We did have a lot of fun doing the show bantering back and forth about family and giving cooking tips," said Shirley. "I don't think I would want to do it all the time, but once in a while would be fun."

"You know what you should do," said Gladys. "Have different family and friends guest with you. The audience would get a feel for who you really are. It would break up the monotony of the same old thing."

"That could work. Mom and I could plan everything in advance, on a schedule of course." They all laughed at that.

"If I want time off, then we would just substitute other family or friends to step in," said Jill feeling the first bit of excitement she had in weeks. "We could even have Nana on the show. After all, she has always been my inspiration."

"How do you think the customers will do without Mountain Mama? After all, she is the gist of the place. Will you still dress up in the band?" asked Gladys.

"You know," said Jill, "I've been doing that part so long, I think I need a change. I could do it once in a while, but I'd like to get away from it full time."

Lorraine came over to join them bringing a platter of homemade breads and jams.

"I heard part of your conversation, Jill, and I think you're on to something. Nana is a lot better with her memory since she decided to try the new medication. I know she'd like to help in some way. Even if it's small."

Nana came in and brought Lorraine the mail. "I've caused ye so much trouble not givin' you the mail and I'm a gonna try to make it up to ye, I am. I'd like to help ye if I can."

Matt had wandered into the room followed by Jim and they had caught part of the conversation as well.

"Think for a minute, ladies," said Matt. "What does Nana do best these days?" They all looked around trying to come up with an answer.

"Well, that's a fine hidy do. The young 'un has to come up with an answer and the rest 'o ye just a sittin' there with yer thumbs a twiddling…I declare!"

Matt just stared at them. "Well?"

"You're the genius," said Jim. "You tell us."

"You just heard it! What Nana does best is interact with people just by being herself. She's witty, she's funny and people love her," said Matt.

"You know, he's right," said Jill. "Remember at the last family band night, she was wandering through the tables chatting with everyone. The customers loved it. Nick told me…" She trailed off. "Nick told me that she was a riot. We wouldn't script anything, just let Nana be Nana!"

"Let's do it," said Jim and Lorraine together. "The next family night is Friday after Thanksgiving. Nana, are you up for this?"

"'O course I am. That's what I like. Just a talkin' to the people. You 'uns always make me sit down and shut up, you do. I can dress like Mountain Mama like I used to," said Nana.

"We might have one problem," said Lorraine. "Mark can't come up. Nancy has been put on bed rest for the rest of her pregnancy. I said I'd keep it quiet, but we're all family and the more prayers, the better." They all said a prayer.

"So we need a drummer," said Jill. "Matt, I guess that'll have to be you."

"Can Annie handle the fiddle on all the songs you all play?" asked Shirley.

"Let's ask her, here she is now," said Matt.

"What do you think Annie, can you do all the fiddle parts for family night?" asked Matt.

"Sure'" she responded. "I probably need to run through some of the music, Matt, since we haven't been practicing lately, but I should have no problem."

"That just leaves us without a piano player," said Lorraine.

"What's wrong with you?" asked Jim. "Are your hands broken?"

"Oh no," said Lorraine not quite meeting their eyes. "My carpel tunnel is acting up and my doctor said I have to lay off the piano for a while...and no air hockey or... cleaning fish either."

"Carpel tunnel? Since when do you have carpel tunnel?" said Jim.

"Cleaning fish and air hockey?" said Gladys with disgust.

Lorraine kicked them both under the table.

"You all know exactly when that happened. It was on the same day that the thing happened when Bam McGee came to the back door..."

"My dad could play," said Anika interrupting.

"That's a wonderful idea," said Shirley.

"Yes, it is," said Lorraine. "I would never have thought of it. Thank you Anika."

Matt rolled his eyes. "You could just ask him, mom, instead of making up that convoluted story."

"Lorraine, honey chile, even this ol'gal could smell that polecat a stinkin' a mile away," said Nana laughing and slapping her thigh.

"I'm serious," Lorraine continued making a show of her aching wrist. "I have to rest it."

"Fine," said Jill. "Brenda will be out of town, too. I'll text Nick about it and see if he can stop by here later to discuss it." She began to text on her phone.

"His time for practice will be limited," said Matt. "He and I are leaving in the morning for the recording session."

"Dad can do it. He's a quick study. The music won't be a problem," said Anika. "Just the style."

"He's not answering," said Jill. "Usually he answers right away. Is he at the job site? I didn't think he would be this late. There's not much that can be done this time of evening."

"No, there's not," said Nick entering the room and seeing his daughter for the first time in nearly a month.

He and Anika looked at each other and very slowly she walked towards him and threw herself into his arms.

Twenty-One

The next week flew past. Nick and Matt had spent four days in New York recording the three songs which would be part of Nick's new CD. Nick had seen nothing of his mother but had dinner at Marcel's with Gwen and they all had gone to the piano bar to see the performance of Brenda's sister, Georgia. That had been a lot of fun.

After their return to Beaumont, Nick had concentrated on learning 'mountain style' music as he called it. Matt had been over almost every day and Anika had moved back home with Nick.

Jill and Brenda were there today and they were all practicing except Brenda who was supervising as she called it. He was doing a great job, but something was missing as Jill kept saying.

"You know, woman, you're the only one I've ever had criticize the way I play the piano," said Nick laughing. He and Jill had found a tenuous friendly relationship in the last week and he didn't want to blow it.

"Then you can make me the second," said Brenda sitting off to the side helping herself to the basket of homemade bread, corn muffins, and assortment of jams made by Aunt Gladys.

"You're lacking flavor," said Brenda. "The playing is fine, but the interpretation lacks. Are you feeling it, Nick?"

If only Jill had been the one to say that to him. Well, maybe not in front of all these people.

"I guess... not entirely. I'm not sure what to do," he said.

They had come to a halt and were just sitting there when the door opened and in walked Gerard and Rod.

"Hey guys! I was wondering when you would turn up! I thought maybe we'd have to have our first Thanksgiving together without you. Did Gwen come?" asked Nick.

"She went over to your place, Jill. Said she thought you wouldn't mind if she stayed with you since Annie moved back home," said Rod.

"No problem," said Jill.

"What's wrong?" Gerard looked around at each face.

"You all look like you're at a funeral." Then he saw Brenda. "Never mind, I see the problem."

"How does such a good looking man about town get to be such a nasty piece of work?" said Brenda.

"Takes one to know one," said Gerard.

"Oh, what fun," said Rod. "I'm going to take the bags up to our rooms.

"Okay," said Gerard. "But leave Jill here, she's practicing. Brenda's enough of a bag for one trip."

"Nasty is as nasty does," said Brenda without batting an eye.

"Then you must be queen," said Gerard sitting opposite her.

"Ooh, baby, don't say it like that!" She leaned forward and blew him a kiss shutting Gerard down with ease.

"Brenda, Gerard, if you don't mind we're trying to solve a problem here," said Nick.

"Let's try again," said Matt. "And this time, try to think country."

They tried 'Take Me Home Country Roads' but it still wasn't there.

"I'm surprised he can play at all in those stuffy designer clothes. He looks like he's off to a court hearing rather than the local watering hole," said a bored Gerard.

"That's it!" Brenda jumped up. "He needs to look the part to play the part. I'll be right back. I've got some of daddy's farm clothes in the back of my car." She ran out the door and came back in carrying a bag of smelly farming clothes.

"My dad's bigger around and shorter than you are but that'll help the overall effect. Come on up to the bedroom and I'll get you out of those clothes and into these," said Brenda.

"I beg your pardon," said Jill a little miffed.

"Well, girlfriend, you're not doing it, so why shouldn't I or any other girl for that matter."

"I'll go and chaperone," said Gerard.

"How old are you people, anyway. You're acting like a bunch of kids. No offense, Miss Montgomery," said Anika.

"I'll have you know, I am thirty six years old," said Gerard arrogantly.

"Well, I'm twenty six, so come on Grandpa, if you insist," and the three headed upstairs.

Fifteen minutes later, Nick returned looking like an out of work hobo walking the railroad tracks looking for cigarette butts.

He sat at the piano looking a little shell shocked.

"Brenda is something else. She nearly ripped my clothes off. I had to stop her and barely made it into the bathroom to change." He shook his head to clear it.

"Where did she go?" asked Jill.

"She was tackling Gerard to the mattress when I escaped," said Nick. "He's probably squirrel bait by now."

They started to practice in earnest and Nick found that the costume really did help. They were just finishing when Brenda came back down the stairs. She looked a little disheveled and Jill took her to the side to ask what on Earth she had been thinking.

"I'm just having fun, girlfriend. I think I just conquered Gerard. He's more fun than I would have thought," said Brenda with a wink.

"I have to run. Me and my folks are leaving first thing in the morning to spend Thanksgiving with Bonnie and Georgia in Chicago. See you next week!" She left jogging out to her car.

Matt and Jill said goodbye and left just as Rod and Gerard came back down stairs.

"She really did that?" Rod was making a face. "What a skank."

"Did what?" Nick left the piano bench.

Gerard walked them through everything Brenda had done while he was in Nick's room.

"Gross!" Nick was disgusted. "I have to sleep in that bed. What were you thinking, man?"

"Hey, I kept my clothes on. Almost all my clothes on." And they started to laugh and make jokes the rest of the evening.

~

They had eaten Thanksgiving dinner at Jim and Lorraine's house along with their father. He told them he had bought a small house near there, a little farther down Turkey Run road. His plan was to build a larger home and possibly retire there.

"Oh, and I forgot to tell you all, Alphonse says we don't need to write any magazine or newspaper article about him any longer. He thinks enough has been said about the whole thing already. He would like to visit your kitchen here, Jill, if you are okay with that," said Andrew.

"Andy, I guess that's fine with me, if that's really why he's coming," said Jill.

"I'll let him know later today."

That had been the best Thanksgiving Nick and Anika had spent in many years. Gerard had been uncharacteristically pleasant. He would thank Brenda, one of these days.

The next evening those playing in the band were assembled in the studio and going over the evening's format. They were dressed in hillbilly clothing and Nick had added a set of fake crooked teeth that had made Jill laugh out loud. He took them out until show time. He was amazed at how well he and Jill were doing at being just friends and although he wanted more, he would take what he could get.

Jill had been a little mad at how Brenda had acted at Nick's house and was glad her friend was not present for this show. She was used to her friend's crudeness but she was a little too loose for Jill. She had not heard details of what happened but she could guess. Maybe Nick would tell her.

"Nick, so what really happened with Brenda and Gerard the other night?" asked Jill in as calm a voice as she could muster.

"I'm not sure I can tell you, but his disposition has been a lot better since then," said Nick.

"Can you whisper it?" She continued to cajole him.

He leaned over and whispered in a few words what had happened.

"She didn't!" cried Jill. "Wait until I get my hands on her. What was she thinking?"

"BAM!" They all heard at the same time.

"Guess who's here?" Matt was calming Anika.

Then they heard what no one was prepared for.

"Make way, make way! Alphonse is in the house!" Into the room pranced Alphonse Laurant as haughty as ever. He went straight to Jill, kissed her hand and then her cheeks. He looked at all the others dressed up in costume.

"What kind of hillbilly hell is this?" He was looking at each person with a look of utter diagust.

Jill briefly explained what was going on and ushered him to a seat usually reserved for family right in front. Nana came over and looked him up and down.

"Sit yer britches on down and shut yer yap. Marlene! Darlene! Come over here an handle this Jack Ass."

Alphonse's face lit up when the two beauties came to sit, one on each side of him.

"Okay, show time," said Andy.

Jim introduced Alphonse to the audience as a special guest and the audience response was tremendous. Even Alphonse was shocked. The internet video had made a star out of him and he hadn't even been in it!

The show was great as usual and Nick had so much fun he couldn't wait to do it again. Nana had worked the audience like a pro and they had loved it.

They were all gathered in the studio talking over what went on when Nana came up to them.

"Andy, they's some folks out front a lookin' to talk with ye if ye have a minute."

"Who is it, Miss Lena?" Andrew asked.

"Bertha Better'n You and …… Roy," she said scratching her chin.

"Roy?" Andrew said.

Nick was kidding around with Jill. He put his teeth back in and pulled up his high water pants as high as he could get. He put his straw hat back on and prepared to greet the new guests.

"Come on pappy, let's us go meet Bertha and Roy."

Andrew hitched up his pants and put his straw hat on.

"I think I know who this is and it's the moment I've been waiting for since I got here."

They strolled out arm in arm, taking big steps as they went, with the rest of the family and Alphonse right behind them.

Standing in the foyer at the front of the restaurant was Margaret and Dr. Weir.

Andrew just grinned at Margaret's shocked, white face and he nodded to Dr. Weir who nodded back.

Nick stepped forward and threw out his arms.

"Mammy!"

At the same time, they all heard behind them a loud "BAM!"

Margaret Wallace screamed and fainted dead away in the floor.

Twenty-Two

The waiting room was packed with Dennison's and Wallace's at Raleigh General's ER in Beckley. Margaret was going to be admitted for observation in the psych ward after the attending doctor's conversation with Andrew and Dr. Weir. Most were talking in small groups waiting to hear any kind of news. At this time, only Andrew and Dr. Weir were allowed to see her.

"I think I can help," said Nana stepping forward.

"Nana, now is not the time. You don't even know Mrs. Wallace," said Jill a little on the irritated side at the moment.

"Hesh up, young 'un. I knowed Maggie Tooley from a way's back, I did. I helped her then and I can help her now."

The attending doctor received permission from Andrew and Dr. Weir for Nana to visit Margaret to the surprise of everyone present. Lorraine and Jim had gone to the cafeteria for coffee so Jill and Nick were elected to escort Nana to the room in the psych ward to which Margaret had been taken.

Walking down the hallway they could hear loud moaning coming from somewhere deeper in the locked area.

"Sounds like a bunch o' haints," declared Nana.

"Haints?" Nick was speaking quietly to Jill so as not to disturb Nana who was clearly on a mission.

"West Virginia for ghosts," replied Jill equally as quiet.

When they reached Margaret's room, Dr. Weir tried to keep them from entering, but too late, they saw the pitiful sight that she made in the hospital bed. She lay curled up in the fetal position and the moans they had heard were coming from her.

Nana looked at Andrew. "Just like before, Andy."

"Yes, Miss Lena, just like before," he agreed.

Margaret began to swat at her face and pull at her hair as her moans turned into screams. She was pulling out big chunks of it when Dr. Weir turned to Nana.

"Go ahead and try."

Andrew saw Jill and Nick still at the door to the room and motioned for them to enter but had them stand back away from the bed. Jill had tears running down her face at the sight of the pitiful woman in so much mental pain that she could barely stand to watch. She put her arms around Nick and buried her face in his shoulder. He put his arms around her and she could feel the emotion coursing through him as well.

Nana slowly approached the bed.

"Maggie, Maggie Magpie, where's my girl?" She spoke slowly in a sing song voice.

"It's me, Miss Lena, come to make it all better."

She motioned for Andrew to get her the rolling stool and she sat closely, near Margaret's face. She quietly stroked her hair and sang softly.

"Turkey in the hay, turkey in the straw. Tie a red ribbon 'round turkey's hind paw. Kick up a tune called turkey in the hay, turkey in the straw..." and the song repeated over and over with the same words.

The song was a favorite from Jill's childhood. She could remember Nana singing it to her when she was hurt or frightened.

Gradually Margaret stopped pulling at her hair and Nana was able to take hold of her hands. The moaning lessened and they could hear Margaret trying to say a few words from the song here and there.

Jill looked around and saw tears on Andrew's face and Dr. Weir was wiping the corner of his eye as well.

Margaret was too weak to sing the song, so she started humming while Nana kept singing. Her eyes remained closed.

Gradually, as Margaret calmed, Nana switched the song to 'Jesus Loves Me'. Maggie switched to humming along with Nana to this song, too, until she drifted off to sleep.

Andrew came over to speak quietly to Nick and Jill.

"Nick, I know you don't understand any of this, but I promised you I would explain some things to you when the time was right. Well, son, that time has come. But not tonight, though. Please take Miss Lena and let everyone know Margaret will be okay for now. I would like for you to gather your brothers and your sister tomorrow morning at Mountain Mama's. After I make sure your mother can do without me for a couple of hours, I will join you for a much needed explanation of many things, so many things."

Jill and Nick walked with Andrew back to the waiting room. Andrew's steps were heavy and he appeared to have aged ten years in the last hour. When they arrived, he called Jim and Lorraine over and explained what would take place.

"Of course we'll be there, Andy," said Lorraine. "We can help fill in the gaps of this complicated puzzle that I am sure your family knows nothing about."

Andrew stepped over to Jill.

"Jill, love, I'd like for you to be present too. You are very important to my son and you deserve to learn the truth, just as they do."

"I'll be there. I'll do anything you say, Andy." She gave him a hug and a kiss on the cheek.

Andrew left to return to his wife. Slowly the Dennison and Wallace clans departed to return to their own homes but not before a heartfelt group prayer for Margaret's recovery and for strength in all of the Wallace's for what would be brought to light the following day.

~

The air was thick with tension the following morning as the Wallace's and Dennison's met in the smaller banquet room upstairs at Mountain Mama's. Jill had felt, due to the solemnity of the occasion, it was better to be behind closed doors for what was about to be revealed.

The kids had not been invited to join and Josie elected to remain with them in the main restaurant keeping to business as usual. Gladys and Shirley had remained in the kitchen as well, keeping that end of the business moving, as it should, without Jill's presence.

Jill had ordered a continental style breakfast rather than heavy food as she had no idea how intense this meeting would be. Some were sitting at the tables eating and talking waiting for Andrew's arrival.

Nick was talking to Jim and Lorraine and Jill decided to join them. Gerard was foregoing any food and was nervously pacing the floor ignoring most everyone. Rod and Gwen were quietly talking and Nana was sitting alone at a table with her head bent, clearly in prayer.

When Andrew entered, all eyes turned towards him. Jill noticed that Dr. Weir was not with him this time. He walked to the front of the room, a very serious look on his face and

Jill's gut took a nose dive at what must be devastating information about to be revealed.

Andrew called Jim, Lorraine and Nana to the front as they were the principle players in what was about to unfold. To their surprise, Jim was the one who started the ball rolling.

"I think some background is in order before we get into other things. I know my family knows most of my background but certainly not all that transpired while I was at the boy's home." He cleared his throat and squeezed Lorraine's hand.

"I was brought into the home at the age of fourteen. I had a great set of parents but no brothers or sisters. Both my parents were only children as well and my grandparents on both sides had passed away at a fairly young age. My father liked to garden and one morning was out early weeding when he fell over. My mother yelled for me to run to the neighbor's house and get help while she ran to help my dad. I've never run so hard in my life. When I got back to the yard, the fire department and local police were there and I saw my mother on the ground beside my father. I tried to run to them but one of the firemen grabbed and held on to me. You see, when my mother ran to my father, she rolled him over and the rattlesnake that killed him, bit and killed her too. I had nowhere to go, so the authorities took me to the boy's home. The day after I arrived, Andrew arrived as well. That was the day both of our lives changed forever.

"I'd never seen such a pitiful two as them there young 'uns. Both fourteen and full of hate and fear. I was the cook at the home but me an' my girls lived purty close, just a stone's throw from the back door. If one o' the young 'uns yelled, I'd a come a runnin', I would," said Nana.

"Once I got 'em cleaned up, they weren't too shabby. They wasn't too many rules in them days 'cept not to go a lookin' fer trouble, and to stay away from the house down the holler, the Tooley house. O'course, that was like a settin' food on the table and sayin' leave it alone."

Andrew took a deep breath.

"Boys and Gwen, what I am about to say will come as a big shock to you all, but you need to sit here and hear me out, until the whole thing is done. And let me apologize to each one of you now, just in case."

He shifted around as the group started to look at each other and Gerard started to look around for the nearest escape. Jill knew then why Andrew had said what he did. Nick took her hand and she was grateful.

"I was born and raised in a little West Virginia town, on the Ohio border, Galipolis. I come from one of only three Amish families to settle in West Virginia proper," said Andrew as he gauged the reaction of his children.

"Amish?" Gerard yelled as he jumped up waving his arms. The others were shocked as well. Jill felt Nick shift in his seat.

Andrew waved his hand and commanded Gerard to sit back down and let him finish.

"I will answer any questions you have after I get this all out. Anyway, the Amish are a wonderful people and do many wonderful things for others. They just like to keep to themselves and live a simple life away from the evils of the world. Unfortunately, my Ordnung was'nt like that. We were ruled with an iron fist and my brothers and sisters felt that fist most every day of our lives, both from our father and the elders that were the head of the church. And my father was the pastor. He used to beat us with belts, shoes, sticks, anything he could get his hands on. We didn't have to do anything wrong to get beat. One day he hit me in the head with a two by four and I was out for a couple of days. My mother was powerless to fight him. All the women were. When I came around, only by the grace of God, I knew I had to get away. I was twelve at the time. I tried to get my siblings and mother to come with me, but they all refused. They all said it wasn't God's will. As soon as I could stand and walk without dizziness, I left with just the clothes on my back. I spent the next two years living on the streets. When I was fourteen, I was picked up by the police for stealing some bread and apples from an old ladies grocery bag when her back was turned. She called the police and I was close enough to Meadow that they took me to the boy's home there. I had told them that my family was dead. I have wondered all these years what happened to my family. I had three sisters and four brothers. About fifteen years after I left, I went back to see if I could find them, but the Amish had moved out of the area. There were some police records that spoke of abused Amish children but no record as to the disposition thereof."

Jill felt so bad for the shock to the Wallace's. Nick was visibly disturbed and Gerard could hardly sit still. Rod had tears on his face as did Gwen.

Lorraine picked up the story from there.

"There was a big house down at the end of Tooley road. I guess more of a mansion. Oscar Tooley, a coal mining magnate, had been married to Belinda, who had died with the birth of her second daughter. Now Belinda had been an alcoholic and her daughter was born with what we know today as fetal alcohol syndrome. They had another daughter that was about a year old at the time. She was small and neglected. Oscar was in no way a person who should have had two babies to take care of. Belinda came from old money herself, so when she died, Oscar was richer than ever. He had the presence of mind in the early days to hire help to raise the girls. He was very fond of the older girl but blamed the younger girl for his wife's death. Both girls were 'failure to thrive' children but the youngest one, was the worst. She was very small and not as pretty as the older girl, so she was told. The oldest girl had honey blonde hair and was beautiful in the face whereas the youngest had brown hair and was more angular in bone structure. She was so small, she looked half her age."

Andrew continued. "In case you haven't figured it out, these girls were Margaret and Bess Tooley, your mother and aunt. What you will hear next will be shocking and hard to listen to, but I think you need to hear it."

Jill felt Nick brace himself and saw the others shift in their seats as well. Nana had her head down, still in prayer, thought Jill.

"The girls grew up despite their neglect and as they did, Oscar got meaner. When they were about nine and ten, he started having more and more parties doing gambling, drinking, drugs, women, you name it," said Andrew.

Nana joined back in. "About a year later, right around the time Andy and Jim came to the home, we 'uns heard screams a comin' from the house and I called the po-lice, I did. I went out into the back yard to see what I could and saw the po-lice a comin' and a goin' too quick to of done a thing. I marched down that holler a carryin' my baseball bat jest in case, you see. About half way down the holler I heard a cry and found Maggie beat up right bad. She had a broken nose with blood drippin' from it and one eye swollen shut. A hunk o' her hair had been ripped clean out.

She was a tremblin' from head to toe. I picked her up and carried her to my house. When she could talk a little, I asked her about her sister and she said she didn't know but didn't think she had been harmed. We kept her with us a while and 'ventually the po-lice came and took her back home. See, ole' Oscar had a lot of clout in them days and the po-lice listened to him 'stead o' the other way 'round."

Jim took up the story from there. "We used to have sing-a-longs back at the home and the girls would stop by after school on most days to join us. Oscar spent more and more time drunk with his parties but on the surface, for those that didn't' live near him, he kept it looking like he had a perfect little family. Bess was allowed to take dance lessons and she also played the violin. She loved to dance and was very good at it. The violin, not so much. Maggie was a child prodigy on the piano. Oscar would invite people over on occasion to watch the girls play piano and dance. She would play for us here almost every day. It was her life. He spent a lot of time and effort to cover his tracks. Every so often Maggie would have bruises on her face or her head with patches of hair missing, but never Bessie. She was always perfect."

"Mother plays the piano and aunt Bess played the violin? I never saw mother near a piano and aunt Bess never mentioned it either," said Nick dumbfounded.

"Let us finish the story, Nicolai, and I think you'll understand," said Andrew.

Nick settled back down and Jill put her arm around him. He gave her a kiss on the top of her head.

Andrew continued. "Jimmy and I got into the habit if we didn't see the girls walking to the bus stop, Miss Lena would let us sneak up to their house to see if things were okay. Oscar was very partial to Bessie and started to think of her more like a wife and Maggie more like a punching bag. As time went on, the girls stopped coming by after a while but the screams coming from the house were getting worse. More and more cars would travel to and from the house until we noticed the girls had stopped going to school. More than once, Miss Lena would find Maggie curled up into a ball in the woods moaning, bloody and bruised. But never on her hands, mostly her face and ribs."

"I don't understand," said Nick. "Why was Mother beaten up and Bess never touched?"

"Nick, this will be particularly hard for you to hear because she raised you, but Bessie didn't go untouched," said Andrew sadly.

"Her scars were internal. He raped her almost every day. He used her as he would a wife and used Maggie as an outlet for his rage at his wife's death because of her birth. He never raped Maggie and he never hit Bessie."

Twenty-Three

Nick put his head in his hands and sobbed. Jill put her arms around him and sobbed with him. It seemed everyone in the room was crying as well.

Andrew rubbed his hands over his face and hair. "I think I am almost finished if you can bear with me a little longer. Like I said, Miss Lena found Maggie several times."

"When I'd find her she'd be almost dead or so I was a thinkin'. I would hold her and sing to her and she would usually come around so's I could get her cleaned up and treat her injuries. But they'd always take her back to that house. I'd spent time with both girls telling them about God and how he can save them, but they never got the chance to go to church and when I gave them a bible, it turned up on my doorstep ripped apart."

"The last day they were in that house, Jimmy and I had come up with a plan to rescue them if we saw a party was going on. That afternoon, we saw more cars than ever going down the road. We waited in the bushes to watch for a while and saw a lot of drunken men wandering around. They were laughing and throwing beer bottles all over the place. There was a younger boy we had seen around town there and the men were pushing him around and calling him 'retard' and some other names. They were telling him he wouldn't be a retard any more if he would have sex with Bessie. He would be a man. They brought Bessie out and tried to force the boy on her but he wouldn't cooperate. He was crying and they started punching him around. Then they brought Maggie out and the men took turns punching her and raping Bess right out in the open with Oscar laughing and egging them on. We had planned with Miss Lena if we didn't return in twenty minutes, to call the police again. Jimmy tried to run in to stop them but I had to hold him back. They would have killed us all. We both started praying and Miss Lena showed up with a first aid kit. The boy was badly beaten by this time and Maggie was almost dead. We heard sirens in the distance and the men started to scatter but Miss Lena had written names down. Before the police got down the road, Oscar went over to Bessie and spit on her bloody legs. Then he took a hammer and crushed Maggie's fingers on both hands and took a good couple of whacks to her forearms. He looked over at the boy who was cowering by Maggie as she screamed over and over. He kept saying "Hit her and I won't set fire to you both, come on, be a man." Then he dumped a bottle of gasoline to Maggie's head and dropped a match on her. She couldn't move her arms to hit at the flames so the boy tried to put out the fire just as the police pulled up and saw the end of it. The police tried to pull the boy from her and he kept saying over and over..."

Andrew looked at them with tears in his eyes. He swallowed hard, and said, "BAM."

Jill gasped. Nick was in shock as were most of the others. Rod cried openly. Gerard had his head in his hands.

"I've got to get out of here," he said, and stood to leave.

"No, son," said Andrew. "I know what you think you need and you don't. We still have talking to do."

"You're telling me that I was descended from an abusive Amish grandfather and a murderous sociopathic rapist? How am I supposed to take this? How are any of us supposed to take this?" Gerard was yelling now.

Nick sat up and didn't bother to dry off his face.

"That's why mother always wore gloves," and his face crumbled into tears again.

"She had the most difficulty being around you, Nick. She loved you very much. She loved all you kids, but she couldn't seem to get it together as a mother. She spent two years in a hospital after that last day. Numerous surgeries to her face and hands. Incredible pain and terrible guilt. Terrible guilt with both girls. They both felt like they were to blame for what happened to the other. Bessie spent a couple of months in the hospital but because of the rapes, she was never able to have children. The trauma she suffered with all the rapes caused many infections rendering her sterile. She had tried to lure her father away from hurting Maggie by using her body. Maggie tried to take the blows to keep him from raping Bessie. It was a 'no win' scenario for them both. But getting back to you, Nick," continued Andrew.

"Your mother would have been as good a piano player as you are and she couldn't bear to hear you play. It brought back memories of what had happened to her."

"Why did she send Gerard and me away?" asked Nick.

"Your mother and I were married after she got out of the hospital. Oscar was convicted and sentenced to death along with some others who participated that night. We had discussed our backgrounds and whether or not we should even try to procreate but we decided to let God decide our future. Bessie met Leonard Brighton and they married and moved to his hometown in New York. Your mother wanted never to lay eyes on West Virginia again or anyone from there. When Oscar was murdered in prison after only serving a few years, the girls inherited all his great wealth. But the girls kept their distance from each other. Maggie felt such great sadness over Bessie not being able to have children. She carries that guilt with her to this day. And she turned from God. She became bitter and started repressing her painful memories. Bessie on the other hand, turned to God and kept her wealth to use only for helping others. She lived off the money she earned with her dance studio. Margaret became pregnant with Gerard and we were so happy. But she had been on medication to help with depression and she couldn't take it while she was pregnant. She had terrible mood swings from manic happiness to deep, dark depression. Gerard took the brunt of that and we could see what an unhappy child he was. We made the hard choice to send him to the best boarding school we could find and he was happy to go."

"Why did you just dump me and leave me there never to hear from you again?" Gerard asked in an angry tone as he got up to pace.

"I didn't. I was in close contact with your teachers every week. Sometimes more often. I was at as many of your sporting events that I could make. The only reason I couldn't make some was when your mother was having more surgery to repair her structural damage. I was at your high school graduation, your college graduation, and your graduation from law school."

"So why was I not aware of this?" Gerard had stopped pacing and had his hands balled into fists.

"I was raised Amish. I felt I had to honor your mother's wishes. We decided to have minimal contact from both of us so you children would not put all the blame on her. When she was well, she was heartbroken, and when not so well, hospitalized under psychiatric care," said Andrew.

"So how did I get to be with Aunt Bess?" Nick was very pale as he spoke.

"Bess couldn't have children and your mother felt guilty about that. We tried to send you to boarding school with Gerard but the two of you didn't get along and you refused to comply with the rules. Your mother had noticed your ability on the piano but couldn't bear to hear you play. She did the best thing she could in her own mind. She asked Bess to raise you as her own and facilitate your gift on the piano. The rest of that is history. Bessie got the opportunity to raise two children, a chance she never would have had otherwise. And, Nick, I met with Bess every week to keep up with how you were doing. And I have been at every concert you have ever performed."

"I never knew dad. I have come to learn just how self-centered I really am. There have probably been lots of things I have missed by not looking around," said Nick sadly.

"By the time Rod and Gwen came along, your mother was a little better and we decided to try to keep them closer than the two of you. Of course, our contact was still basic, I'm sad to say. I should have done the right thing and been a real father to you but, I guess, I did what I thought was right at the time."

Andrew was wiping his eyes. "Gwen and Rod, I was also at everything you accomplished as well."

Gwen spoke. "I know father, I saw you sometimes, and I heard you singing to mother once in a while. I always thought there was more to the story. I wish I had asked more questions and tried harder with mother. But even though Rod and I grew up in the same penthouse, we rarely interacted, so it's not like he and I had an advantage over you guys," she said to Gerard and Nick.

"One more thing," said Andrew. "Your aunt Bess was at most of your functions as well, not just Nick's and Anika's. I'm sure you all realize that she didn't just leave her money to Nick and Anika. I know you all received gifts too."

The Wallace's looked at each other. Finally, Rod spoke with a catch in his voice.

"The jet came from her, didn't it?"

"Yes, son, it did."

"I just thought I was lucky. Dumb huh," said Rod.

"I received a Maserati and enough diamonds and jewels to sink a ship," said Gwen.

"I received two stays in the finest rehab facility in the world and my own club," said Gerard.

He saw the others staring.

"Long story, now's not the time."

Silence reigned in the room along with a few sniffles here and there. Finally, Lorraine stood up.

"I think we have all had enough for one day. I know I have. Help yourselves to anything you want to eat and I suggest you all take some time to think over what has been shared here today. The thing I hope you all come away from this with is that everything is not always as it seems on the surface. The potential for so much love is in this room today. I challenge all of you to embrace it and not throw it away." She looked at Nick and Jill when she said the last part.

Twenty-Four

For the next two weeks, Margaret remained in the psychiatric ward at Raleigh General. Andrew had told the families that he could have had her transferred to New York to her usual hospital but felt she could get the same treatment here.

Several months ago, he had devised his own brand of therapy which had all rested upon his returning to West Virginia and forcing Margaret to return as well. When he had found that Bam McGee was still in the area, he and Dr. Weir discussed the best way to get her here in the hopes that seeing Bam and seeing Nana would cause the long buried emotions to surface so they could be dealt with. In all of her prior hospitalizations, they had only given her drugs to help her cope. They had tried therapy numerous times, but she would not continue the sessions more than a few times.

Dr. Weir had told Andrew that until she chose to get and continue help, she would continue down her destructive path. She had attempted suicide on four different occasions and Andrew had felt that the only one with which she had ever felt safe, was Nana.

Nick had been hiding away in his house over the past couple of weeks trying to come to terms with the truth versus what he had believed to be the truth. Rod had been there with him as well, but Gwen and Gerard had returned to their own homes.

Gerard had been a mess and the family had prayed for him daily. Nick suspected he was drinking way too much and the questions about his rehab statement remained unanswered.

Nick had allowed Anika to stay with Jill and to let Jill explain the events to she and Matt. Nick did not think he could do it. He had made sure to call Jill every day to see how things were going and he felt that his friendship with Jill had become stronger than ever. However, the romantic side had not returned.

Jill had told him she was having Alphonse on her show to try another demonstration segment for the end of this series of shows. It would be a Christmas show and, she hoped, her last as Mountain Mama. That would happen tomorrow evening and he and his family would be there. He had a surprise of his own planned.

His phone rang and he saw it was his dad on the caller ID.

"Hello dad, how is mother?"

"A little better. She will be discharged to my care in the morning. Dr. Weir thinks the best medicine for her at this time is to stay as close to Nana as possible. The Dennison's have put another bed in Nana's room and she will stay there. He wants her to slowly get to know her children as they are today. It's hard to say how that will go," said Andrew. "I'm going to take her to Jill's show tomorrow evening. It'll be a trial run to see how she does in public."

"Is there anything I can do for her?"

"No, son, just be yourself. That is all any of us need to be. Let the Lord work in her and the rest of us. There is a lot of healing that needs to be done in this family," said Andrew a little sadly.

"I am worried about Gerard, though," said Nick. "I think he is drinking too much. He says he's coming back here soon, but who knows."

"I just hope that drinking is all he's doing," said Andrew.

"Hey, I've got to go, but I'll see you tomorrow. I love you son, I always have." And he hung up the phone before Nick could reply.

~

The next afternoon, Jill was in her living room dressed as Mountain Mama, getting ready to go to the studio. Anika and Matt wandered in.

"Jill, do you still love my dad?" Anika appeared very nervous.

Jill was taken aback. Anika had not brought this subject up in a while now. She decided to be honest.

"With all my heart. But sometimes there are problems that keep a relationship from moving forward."

"And just what is the problem, sis? You love him. He loves you. From what I can tell, the chemistry is great."

"LaLaLaLaLa..." Anika had her hands over her ears to keep from hearing any more.

"Anika, knock it off. I'm trying to make a point here. Like mom said, you have the potential for something great. Why would you throw that away over issues that aren't really issues at all?" Matt was letting his frustration show.

"Matt," said Jill. "I know you want to help, but Nick is going through a lot right now and trying to push this relationship back into a romantic one, would not be a big help."

"What if that was what he wanted," said Matt a little too suspiciously for Jill.

"What are you up to, Matthew Dennison? Are you up to something too, Annie Wallace?" Jill started going downstairs.

"Hey, we're both innocent of any interference sis," said Matt as he crossed his fingers and went to stand with the rest of the family.

"I'm just happy my uncles are here," said Anika before she joined Matt. "What are the odds that uncle Gerard would show up again this soon?" She ran to give her uncles a big hug.

When Jill entered the studio, she saw Alphonse waiting for her. She could see Nick and both his brothers in the audience and Gwen standing off to the side with Lance. Her parents were there, and in the front row with Andrew, sat Margaret and Nana.

Nana was holding tightly to Margaret's hands. Margaret was pale and looking a little dazed, but was holding up as well as she could under the circumstances.

Jill took her place behind the kitchen counter and spoke in French to Alphonse to make sure they were on the same page with the show's plan. Alphonse assured her that he understood what was to take place. Jill tried to ignore the grimace on his face as he looked at her in full costume.

The music started and Jill began her hillbilly dance.

"Welcome to 'Cooking Up a Storm' with me, Mountain Mama and I'd like you to give a big welcome to special guest, Alphonse Laurant!"

The audience erupted in enthusiastic clapping and yelling as well as a standing ovation.

They started chanting "Alphonse! Alphonse! Alphonse!"

He was startled at the response but bounded up to the kitchen area and motioned for the audience to settle down.

"Alphonse thanks you all. If not for you, I would not be television star!"

He threw kisses to the audience and a special kiss to Marlene who was standing just out of the camera's reach.

The music started back up and Jill and Alphonse did an impromptu square dance for the audience.

"Today Alphonse is a gonna make y'all a real French supper, and I mean he's a gonna make a good 'un," said Jill. "Good enough fer Christmas supper!"

Alphonse took the lead and explained what he was cooking and demonstrated how to do it. Jill assisted and they bantered back and forth as they did so.

Alphonse was stuffing a duck and he began to tell the story about a time in his youth when he was bitten by a duck.

"I was in my yard and the neighbors had some pet ducks. This one duck kept coming over to my yard almost every day for weeks. This one day I was sitting on my swing and the naughty thing just waddled over and bit me. Anyway, after that, I named it."

"What? The bite or the duck?" Jill wondering what the point of that story was but it got a good laugh out of the audience.

"Oh...Mountain Mama, you are naughty too! You're just trying to get my coat," said Alphonse shaking his finger at Jill.

"Get yer what, Alphonse? Do ye mean 'get yer goat?'"

"Goat? There's goat?" Alphonse looking around.

"I'll be glad to get his goat if it'll move this farce along," said Gerard to Brenda who was standing next to him.

Jill noticed that Nick was moving up towards the front of the audience area near her parents. *What was this?* she thought. He looked like he was about to faint again.

She noticed Brenda had come in and was standing off to the side near Gerard who jumped and yelped. Brenda had clearly pinched him in the rear.

Something was definitely up, she thought. Brenda never came to these things.

"What is your problem?" Gerard looked at Brenda.

"You're like a bad rash I can't get rid of. Every time it pops up, you just have to scratch it," said Brenda.

"It is so hard to believe you're a teacher. You are so unprofessional," criticized Gerard.

"Well, I don't have to be professional unless I'm teaching, but I sure could teach you a thing or two." And she marched off to the other side of the room.

Matt walked over to where Gerard was standing watching Brenda depart.

"Gerard, I know we haven't gotten to know each other very well…"

Gerard interrupted. "And I'd like to keep it that way." He followed Brenda to the other side of the room ignoring Matt's response.

"Ass!".

Alphonse completed his duck Christmas dinner with a flourish. He yelled to the audience.

"I have made special dessert for special occasion." He waved for Marlene to bring him something off stage.

"What do you think you're doing? This was not part of what we talked about. I told you, no changing the plan!"

Alphonse ignored her and continued his speech.

"I'd like to ask another special guest to join us and I think you will recognize him as the fake Alphonse Laurant and as you can see, there is only one real Alphonse. Please welcome Nicolai Wallace anyway, world renowned pianist! Come on up, Nicolai!"

Jill was speechless. What was going on?

"Alphonse! What are you doing? Nick, what is going on?"

She tried to speak without the audience hearing. She could see Nick was sweating and her family was smiling, even Margaret looked a little less dazed.

"I don't know about you folks, but it's a gettin' hot up here. Mountain Mama's got two good lookin' fellers a tryin to court her at the same time. Get yer fancy pants over here and give ol' Mountain Mama a hug, now, both o' ye," she said.

Nick spoke first. "Alphonse has made a special cupcake for this evening just for you Mountain Mama. Anika could you get it from Marlene and bring it here, please? My daughter, Annie, everyone!"

The audience had picked up on the fact something big was going to happen and the applause and noise was deafening.

Alphonse was glowing and throwing kisses to his fans.

Anika brought the cupcake to Nick. She did a curtsy and waved to the audience like she was a model.

"This had better be good boys," Jill said under her breath.

"This is a gonna be special y'all!" Nana yelled. "And I ain't just a whistlin' Dixie!" More applause ensued.

Nick stepped forward and Alphonse took the cake. He held it out to Jill.

"This is very special cake for you to try now. Take a big bite out of it. Go on, take a bite."

"I bet Mountain Mama wants to take a bite, but not of the cake, ain't that right, Nick?" yelled Nana.

He handed the cake to Jill and she took a big bite, nearly choking.

"What the heck?" She spit something into her hand. It was a huge diamond ring.

"Oh!" She gasped. She looked up at Nick.

He took her hand and moved her to stand in front of the kitchen counter so the cameras could catch the whole thing. He wiped the ring off on a napkin and got down on one knee.

"Jillian Marie Dennison, it would be an honor if you would agree to be my wife." The whole audience had gone quiet.

Jill had a thousand thoughts flicker through her mind but the only one that really counted was that she loved this man. That he would propose to her while she was dressed as Mountain Mama and on camera, no less, really made a statement to her.

"Well, 'ere ye or ain't ye girl?" Nana, of course.

"Oui! Yes!" She held out her hand to allow Nick to put the ring on her finger. Nick pulled Jill to him and for a moment they just stared into each other's eyes. Then he pulled her to him for a lingering kiss.

"Hot diggety dog!" Nana was yelling and had pulled Margaret to her feet.

"We're a gonna get us some grandchildren, Maggie, you mark my words! Do it, girl, do it!"

Mountain Mama and Nicolai. Blue Ridge Mountains and New York City, united in love.

Twenty-Five

They had married on Christmas Eve at Jill's church. Anika had served as Jill's maid of honor and Matt had been Nick's best man. Josie, Gwen and Brenda had been brides maids and Gerard, Rod, and Mark were groomsman.

Gwen had thrown Jill a bachelorette party in New York City and Andrew and Jim had thrown a great bachelor party at Gerard's club in Chicago. Lorraine and Nana had thrown a nice wedding shower for Jill a week before the wedding.

The wedding reception was held at Mountain Mama's, of course, and catered by Alphonse Laurant. He had been assisted by Lance and Jean and had been happy with the outcome. He was also very happy with Marlene and they had become an item.

Nick and Jill had been making the rounds greeting all of their friends and family. Finally, Jill had to take a seat to rest her aching feet. They sat at the bride and groom's table where some of the other family members were seated for the same reason. They were joined by Matt and Anika who were discussing Gerard's bad behavior.

"He's a jerk," said Matt very perturbed. "Every time I get near him, he tells me to buzz off."

"Please, change of subject," said Jill.

"So Rod, when did you learn to fly," asked Mark.

"In the Air Force," stated Rod flatly, earning a surprised gasp out of most of the siblings.

"You never told us you were in the Air Force," said Nick with surprise on his face.

"Didn't think about it," replied Rod dumping sugar into his tea.

"Were you ever overseas?" asked Mark calmly.

"I did a tour in Afghanistan, not a big deal."

"Not a big deal?" Josie almost shrieked. "Is there anything else you do that we don't know about?"

"Let's see," said Rod taking a drink of his tea. "I play the accordion."

"What?!" They all spoke at once.

Josie grabbed his hand. "Come on, honey, I'm signing you up for Family Night!"

Nick leaned over for another kiss from Jill.

"That's it, we're out of here!" Anika grabbed Matt's hand and pulled him back out to the dance floor.

Nick pulled Jill to her feet. "Let's go say goodbye to mother and Nana. It looks like dad is getting ready to take them home."

After the goodbye's had been said, Nick pulled Jill to him for another slow dance.

"You are so beautiful, Mrs. Wallace. How did you ever get a wedding of this magnitude ready in three weeks?"

"Never underestimate the power of a few strong-willed women with event planning on their minds," replied Jill.

Gerard was talking with Brenda close by and they heard Gerard getting aggravated.

"This is a public room. What do you think you're doing Brenda?"

"What comes naturally, baby, just what comes naturally," and she grabbed his hand pulling him out to the dance area.

"You know," said Nick. "I haven't slept well since Brenda tackled Gerard on my bed and...you know."

"Yeah, unfortunately, I think everyone knows," she replied.

"I love you so much and I am having a hard time waiting for this reception to be over. I need you more than I can say. You have no idea, woman."

"I have a very good idea. I think we should do something about it right now. I love you and I can't wait any longer. Meet me in my living room in two minutes."

"You know we'll be interrupted. We have been every time we have had a hot make out session together. Won't everyone notice we're gone?"

"Trust me, this time, we won't be interrupted," and she gave him a kiss that promised more.

As she passed the stairs she slipped a fifty dollar bill into the hand of Bam McGee to stand guard and yell real loud if anyone came looking for them.

Nick met her in her living room five minutes later having passed Gerard by the stairs looking dazed and confused. He had probably been attacked by Brenda again, as he almost had a smile on his face.

Nick pulled her down on his lap. She kissed him thoroughly over and over and he let his hands roam over her since, as her husband, he was allowed. He slowly slid her Grecian style white gown down to her waist and found she had nothing on underneath. He feasted his eyes upon her beauty and groaned.

"Babe, I can't wait." And he picked her up and carried her to the bedroom.

A little later, they were lying next to each other, trying to catch their breath.

"Babe, that was incredible!"

"You're telling me! I've never felt like this in my life. I can't get enough of you." She started kissing his incredibly toned chest and abdomen trying to get things going again.

"I think we've pushed our luck as far as we can. We should get back downstairs. We'll have the rest of the night, and the next two weeks in Greece." He kissed each of her breasts, places that were formerly forbidden.

She groaned. "You're right, of course. I'll never stop loving you."

"Nor I, you," he agreed.

And they rejoined their party downstairs and as they cut the cake and were toasted by all their friends and family, they realized how God had taken all they had been through, all their families had been through, and turned it around for good, just as he said he would for those that love him.

Marianne Waddill Wieland

Epilogue

The next day they had spent Christmas with their combined families at the Dennison's home. Margaret had settled in but still had that dazed look about her and said very little to anyone, except Nana. Andrew had said it was due to her medication.

He also announced that she would be retiring from her position as CFO of the Grand Wallace hotels and he asked Rod to step into that position. Rod was glad to accept.

Andrew said that he was planning to retire within the next year and would name his replacement closer to that time.

Anika and Matt kept turning up under the mistletoe and stealing kisses but kept promising they were only friends.

Gerard stuck it out as long as he could and left before dinner was served. He had been antsy and could hardly keep still all day. And Alphonse had invited himself to their Christmas celebration as well, stating he had no family in this country.

Later in the day, Nick and Jill had left on a commercial flight to Greece for their honeymoon. As soon as they got to their hotel room, they made love. And again, and again, and again.

"Babe, I can't get enough of you," said Nick kissing every inch of her.

"My turn," she said.

She pushed him over onto his back and returned the favor by kissing every inch of him. Nick groaned finally and she was very satisfied as was he.

"Do you remember that fateful night in New York after the concert, when I told your ex, Geoff, all those things about you?" Nick asked lazily.

"How could I ever forget that?" She responded in a sleepy voice.

"Well, babe, everything I said is the God's honest truth."

"I'm glad you think so," she said snuggling up to him for a nice nap.

They spent the next two weeks visiting every tourist site and town as well as so many restaurants, Jill lost count.

The last night in Greece, they had made love in the shower and were drying off when Nick's phone rang. He didn't recognize the caller ID, but he answered anyway.

"Nick, it's me, Gerard."

"Oh, how's it going?"

"Shut up, Nick. This is no time for small talk. I only get one phone call. I need you to get in touch with Jim and both of you come to Chicago ASAP. I need help."

"What's wrong?" Nick was alarmed.

"I know I haven't been a good big brother, but I'm in over my head, and I'm asking you, as a brother, to help me," said Gerard in a husky voice.

"Are you okay? I'll be there as soon as I can. It's hard to hear you. The phone is breaking up. Are you at home?"

"No," said Gerard hesitantly.

"Where will I find you?" Nick asked this as he grabbed a pencil and paper to write down the address.

"I'm in jail."

Acknowledgements

I would like to thank Paula Hawkins for being there for me and for reading the entire book as I was writing it. She spent many hours proof reading and giving me input into the story content and characters. I couldn't have done it without her.

I would also like to thank Gladys Barrington for reading the entire book as well. She has been a big fan and gave much encouragement as each chapter developed. Every day she was waiting to see if the next chapter had been finished.

Many thanks to family, friends and co-workers who encouraged me along the way. You were all a blessing.

Marianne Waddill Wieland

Have you ever wished you could have a 'do over'? I think most of us have wished that at one time or another. As I was writing this book, I realized I was writing the life I would have chosen for myself if I had been able to do so. The character of Jill is spunky and independent as well as beautiful, even though she doesn't realize it. I love to cook and would have loved to have run my own restaurant. However, thinking about the hard work, long hours, and time commitment this would take caused my lazy side to kick in. There was no way I could do this and work full time in my regular job. Then I thought, I won't be able to do it, but I can write about it. And so this book began.

My real world is very different from Jill's life. I have been a nurse for thirty- four years and more years than that singing and dancing on stage or behind it directing. My husband, Douglas, and I have taken care of my ninety-five year -old mother for the last six years. She is in the end-stage of Alzheimer's disease and on hospice now but can still make us laugh…and cry. We have raised my two sons, Scott and Steven and a host of various animals. My son, Scott and daughter-in-law, Kirsten, have blessed me with a grandson, Liam.

Although I was born in Beckley, West Virginia, I was raised on the east coast in the tourist town of Williamsburg, Virginia. Twenty-five years ago I moved to the small town of Bellevue, Michigan, where I currently reside. None of the characters in this book are real, but they do consist of bits and pieces of my life and the lives of my family and friends. I hope you enjoy reading my 'do over' as much as I enjoyed writing it. See you at Mountain Mama's!

Made in the USA
Lexington, KY
28 April 2018